Devil's Daughter

FAMILY & FIRE

JANE PEARCE

Order this book online at www.trafford.com
or email orders@trafford.com

Most Trafford titles are also available at major online book retailers.

Print information available on the last page.

ISBN: 978-1-4907-9874-5 (sc)
ISBN: 978-1-4907-9875-2 (hc)
ISBN: 978-1-4907-9876-9 (e)

Library of Congress Control Number: 2019920135

Trafford rev. 12/09/2019

www.trafford.com
North America & international
toll-free: 1 888 232 4444 (USA & Canada)
fax: 812 355 4082

1

oxes were scattered in the tunnels that once held evil. Now a new type of evil was moving in—an accepted evil that had saved everyone. All the evidence for the upcoming trial of Alexander had been moved out of the underground tunnels. It had only been a couple months since the events that led to Alexander's capture, but an overwhelming feeling of calm was already felt throughout the city of Harmon. Just getting the evil bastard off the streets gave the people of Harmon their sense of security back. The citizens had a feeling of safety that hadn't been felt in over twenty years. Ryan was able to get the go-ahead from Chief Doyle on Abby having an apartment belowground. It wasn't a difficult decision when the chief realized it would be easier to have her and her creatures belowground and away from the public's view anyway.

The cold, rough winter had turned to spring, and the city of Harmon was nearing the beginning of summer. The people of

Harmon were finally safe, and their new freedom showed. The garbage that once littered the streets were now replaced with colorful flowers and beds of roses. Beautiful plants hung from the streetlights that were once covered in graffiti. Closed businesses were now reopened, making it easier for people to get jobs. The number of homeless within the city was almost cut in half already. Harmon's Townsquare was back to its normal beauty, and it was always full of people. Visitors from outside cities were actually coming to Harmon now and spending time and money there. The police were able to focus their time on smaller things, like traffic violations and parking tickets—all things needed to bring money back into the city.

Alexander had been held without bail, and his once-loyal hounds were making sure he was held securely. They took shifts and organized themselves in ways that regular animals would never be able to. While a few stayed and guarded Alexander, the rest would come back home to Abby. Alexander's presence was too much for the officers at the regular jail. He was held at a separate facility that was kept unlisted and unknown to the public. Even Abby hadn't been there, not that she was interested in going at all. Chief Doyle had given Abby the address where the dangerous prisoner was being held, but Abby threw it out immediately. She was hoping that part of her life was closed and she could just move on.

"Move, damn it!" Abby heard coming from the hall. Ryan came in, stumbling with the few remaining boxes from the car. "For how intelligent they are, they refuse to move when you need to get by them!" Ryan said loudly, pointing to the hellhounds scattered throughout the underground structure.

"I find that intelligence and stubbornness usually come as a package deal." Abby snickered.

"I'll take your word for it," snapped Ryan.

Abby grabbed one of the boxes from Ryan. "I can grab the rest," she said, putting down the boxes.

"That was the last of them," Ryan added as he placed the other boxes down.

Abby looked around her new home. It was so much bigger than her tiny apartment, and this one was meant to be hers. The huge open room was separated only by style and furniture. As soon as you walked into the room, there was a small sitting area with a TV that hadn't been used yet. The small separate room off to the right-hand side had all of Alexander's items moved out of it and was divided in half. It was now a kitchen with a small bathroom through a separate entrance. Those were the only separate rooms. A huge canopy bed was at the far corner with a couple of small tables and a plush red chair that Abby usually put her coat on. Behind the chair, against the wall, was a small dresser. Abby didn't have much clothing; she never understood the point. Beside the bed, near the bathroom entrance, was a punching bag Abby had set up to work out her anger on. She touched it as she walked by to go to the bedroom portion.

A small purr came from the bed. Hecate was lying on her back, looking at Ryan and Abby. Her adorable small fangs peeked out over her lips. The small black cat had already made herself at home there.

"I still don't understand where she came from," Ryan said as he walked over to the bed.

"I just accepted her. She's so cute!" Abby said, rubbing Hecate's tiny belly. Abby was the happiest she had ever been. She actually had a home—a real home—with a family of creatures that were much more loyal than any mortal family she had encountered. Once the trial for Alexander was over with, Abby could move on and forward. Thinking about the future was still so new to her.

Abby's happiness was cut short when Ryan's beeper went off.

"You have a beeper, old man!?" Abby laughed. Ryan took it out and looked at the number before pushing Abby onto the bed playfully but aggressively.

"It's the only way anyone can get ahold of me down here in your weird place," he said. He looked at the beeper and sighed. "It's the station. I have to crawl up and take a call," he said as he rushed out the door.

Abby fell back onto the bed, smiling. Hecate rolled over without getting up so she was able to look at Abby. Like most cats, she was lazy and didn't like putting much effort into anything. But she was also so much more. Ryan would get a little freaked out by how intelligent Hecate was and how expressive her face was when she looked into anyone's eyes. It was as if she were looking through you or inside you. Either way, all the things that freaked Ryan out about Hecate were the things that made Abby adore her fury little friend.

As much as Abby loved her new life and everything that came with it, she couldn't help but notice that Ryan's attitude and personality had been drastically changing since the events that took place a couple months ago—basically since the moment they met. It wasn't a frightening change from what she could see, but he was acting more and more like Abby each day or like Alexander. Each time Abby thought about it, she just shrugged it off and figured it was because they were spending so much time together. It's common for people to pick up each other's quirks after spending so much time with them, even their humor. But at least he wasn't killing people with fire.

The dogs stirred as Ryan came back in, climbing over them in the doorway. "Seriously, guys," he mumbled.

Abby sat up on the bed where Ryan left her. "We have to go. The chief needs to see us," said Ryan in the commanding voice that always drove Abby wild.

"Yes, sir!" said Abby as she smacked his ass while getting up. "Let me just grab my boots!" She pulled out her old thigh-high boots from under the bed.

"Aren't you going to change?" Ryan asked, smirking. Abby was wearing black tights and a skull-printed tank top that was part of an old pajama set. She had decided to wear something ultra comfortable while unpacking.

"Nope, I'm comfortable. And I'm going somewhere uncomfortable, so this is happening," she said as she tossed on her fake leather jacket.

Just as they got to the door, Abby stopped and looked in the mirror. She grabbed a brush from a small bench under the mirror and ran it through her long red hair. Her hair even shined underground in the dull artificial lighting. The hellhounds at the doorway that wouldn't move for Ryan were quick to adjust their bodies so Abby could get by them. She pet each one of them on the head as she walked by.

In the tunnels just above Abby's living quarters, there were about fifty to sixty dogs scattered about, most of whom were lying down while some were eating from the dishes of raw meat Abby had put out for them. The tunnels were no longer red and gold. All statues and possessions belonging to Alexander had been seized. Even the red shag carpet had been taken up because of the blood and the need for DNA testing to ensure there weren't more victims. It was a plain hallway now. The only style and carpeting was in Abby's room beneath them.

Since certain city officials were aware of Abby living down there, the tunnels had been cleaned up, and a ledge was put in for Abby to walk on in order to exit her home easily without stepping on gross debris. Springtime also made it easier. The slush and ice from winter added so much more mud.

The opening at the back of the grounds that led to Townsquare was closed up after it became public that Alexander had frequently used it; however, the bars at the end of the tunnels that led to the small stream where Abby had fallen into in the winter had been removed, and that area had been resurfaced. Now instead of climbing down the rocks at the side of the tunnel opening to avoid the water, Ryan and Chief Doyle had commissioned a city contractor to put in a sturdy set of metal stairs. It was perfect.

Ryan parked on a small side street that was a minute's walk from the tunnel instead of parking at Townsquare and walking across the grounds. Although he kept his own apartment at their old building, Ryan was spending most of his nights with Abby at her place. Abby got in the passenger side of the car and looked over to Ryan.

"So are you going to tell me what's up, or should I start guessing? We both know how annoying that gets," Abby said to Ryan as he started to drive. He had a stern look of focus that Abby hadn't seen in a while.

"There might be a copycat," Ryan said with disappointment in his face.

"A copycat Alexander?" Abby asked, hoping it wouldn't be confirmed.

"Maybe. Two more girls have gone missing again, and a few regular criminals have been found dead. It looked like one of Alexander's turf killings."

Abby nodded her head in acknowledgment of the information given to her but wasn't sure how to react to it yet. She tried to think it through and looked out the window as they drove by a small park. It was a park she had seen many times before—a place parents would never take their children before, until the recent half after Alexander's arrest. The park used to be full of criminals and trash. But now it was full of kids, and the grass was greener than Abby had ever seen it. There were even older ladies tending to a small community garden they had begun in the beginning of spring—not that Harmon was going into summer. The plants had sprouted, and the older women were looking at the sizes of the tomatoes they grew. Families were having picnics, and men were gathered at a BBQ area while their wives and children played. All this would go away if people were to find out that Alexander's ways were back on the street.

"Are they keeping it quiet so far?" Abby asked finally as she continued to look out the window.

"So far, but you know how easy it is for the media to get ahold of things now," Ryan said as he pulled into the parking lot at the police station.

The pair walked into the station to learn some unsettling news. An officer greeted them at the door and informed them that Alexander had been moved and was now being kept at the newly renovated courthouse to await his trial. The courthouse was full of people he could easily torment, or worse. Abby shook her head, not understanding why they thought this was a good idea. Ryan touched Abby's arm as he left her side and went in to speak with the chief about the circumstances. Abby left the police station when she noticed most of the officers staring at her again. Staring is expected when people don't understand something, but that doesn't make it any less uncomfortable. She decided to walk around outside for a few minutes, enjoying her time aboveground. The roads leading into town that were starting to be covered over with grass from no use were now newly paved, and there was actually traffic coming into Harmon. The city had just been restored, and now there was already a threat that could send it back into darkness. Abby felt so responsible; if she had just killed him, none of this would be happening.

The door to the station flung open. Abby looked over. Multiple cops were running out of the building. Abby watched as many of the cops who were just in the station jumped into their cruisers and sped out of the parking lot. The lot was almost empty now. Abby walked back into the police station to find it also mostly empty. The officers on duty were all out looking for any information on the copycat. The chief looked extremely stressed-out—probably why an officer ran from the station when given his orders.

Ryan and the chief were sitting at a corner desk with another officer listening in. Abby heard one of the officers mention that the girls had been missing for thirteen hours. Once it hit twenty-four hours, their disappearances would be all over the news, and any hope of keeping this quiet would be lost.

"So we ask Alexander," she said, interrupting. All three of the men looked at her like she was insane—nothing she wasn't accustomed to already.

"Would it not be easier to get the information straight from the horse's mouth instead of trying to start from scratch all over again?" Abby said.

The chief stood up and walked over to Abby. "We have no reason to believe he would help us," he said with a curious vibe.

"Oh, no, he won't. Not on purpose anyway," Abby added.

The chief stood there thinking for a moment before Ryan spoke up. "Sir, if you want her to try, we can head downtown now."

Ryan waited for the okay from his superior. Without words, Chief Doyle nodded his head. His mind was spinning. Ryan grabbed Abby's hand and led her toward the door.

"Family reunion?" he joked as he rushed Abby to the car. As they left, a few officers were walking up the steps to enter the station. Their eyes made it obvious they were just getting off a long shift. They looked disappointed in themselves, which led Abby to believe they didn't have any news either.

Ryan tried making small talk as they drove to the courthouse, but Abby was quiet. It had been over three months since she had even seen Alexander. Her life was so much better now, but this almost felt like she was taking a step backward. She was just so excited to move on and forget about Alexander.

"A really annoying bass player moved into your old place," Ryan said, pointing to their old apartment at the corner of the intersection.

They stopped at a red traffic light on the corner. Abby looked at her building, then at the lot across the street. It was still empty; no one was willing to take over Liz's lot just yet. Abby often thought about Liz and of working at Duffy's bar. She regretted not getting closer to Liz and always thought about whether Liz would be alive if she had done something differently. Ryan looked at Abby as her mind wandered while she stared at Duffy's lot.

"You never talk about her. Do you want to?" he asked.

Abby took a moment to snap out of her thoughts. "You don't talk about your family either. It's just easier that way," Abby said. Even as it came out of her mouth, Abby knew that bringing up Ryan's dead family was in poor taste, even for her.

"That's different," Ryan said before Abby could even figure out how to apologize for her words. "I've had over twenty years to process their loss, but you just lost Liz a few months ago."

"You're right, it is different," Abby cut in. "You lost your family. I lost an employer whom I didn't even get close enough to in order to consider her a friend. It's very different."

Ryan drove on, away from the memories for a moment, before chiming in again. "It sounds like you regret not getting closer to her," he said.

I can see why he's a detective, she thought to herself. Even her thoughts were being sarcastic today. Abby looked out the window, doing her best not to get emotional. She had been so happy for the last couple months, and it felt like it was crumbling so quickly.

As they approached the courthouse, Abby could sense Alexander inside. But it wasn't the depressed, ill-powered Alexander they had left a few months ago. Something was different. He wasn't as strong as he was in the winter, but he wasn't as weak as he was before they moved him here. Ryan parked and quickly got out of the car. Abby sat there for a moment with the door closed, listening to her senses. It wasn't long before Ryan realized he was walking alone and turned around to look for Abby. Abby was still inside her head. She was trying to understand how he could be getting stronger from inside a jail cell.

A knock from Ryan on the door window brought her back to reality, and she got out of the car. Ryan looked at her, confused.

"What's going on?" he asked.

"I'm not sure, but something's not right. He's doing better somehow," Abby said, trying to explain what she didn't understand.

"Better?" Ryan asked.

"Yeah. Not a threat yet, but still, he's getting stronger again," Abby continued.

Ryan looked at the courthouse. It was the same red brick it was before, but the whole left side of the building was made of brand-new bricks after being redone. It was very noticeable since the old bricks had been bleached a bit from the climate.

"Should we forget about this meeting?" Ryan asked, looking for direction.

"No," Abby said quickly. "Now we definitely need to know what's going on. Besides, if I can sense him this well, then he can sense me. He already knows we're here." This made Ryan gulp and look around.

Ryan took Abby's hand as they walked up to the large building together. The outside was bright, and the landscaping was beautiful. But as soon as Abby stepped inside the doors, the stench of evil made her feel sick to her stomach. She hadn't felt this sick in months, and hated it. Ryan looked around, and Abby noticed an alarmed look on his face. Her eyes followed his, and she was more than a little creeped out. The people who worked in the courthouse looked like they were all extremely sick. Abby approached a woman working at the front reception desk. Her hair looked like it hadn't been brushed in days, and her eyes had dark circles around them like she hadn't slept either.

"Is there lack of staff for this place or something?" Abby asked with a smile, trying to be friendly.

"No," the woman answered, staring back at Abby blankly. Abby looked at Ryan.

"Your turn," she said, looking back at the woman who was making her feel odd. Her mind was blank. Even the nicest people on the planet had an evil or at least ill-willed thought about something now and then.

"We're here to see Alexander Smith. He's being held for trial," Ryan said, hoping that carrying on with their duties would end this uncomfortable interaction as quickly as possible.

Abby and Ryan stood waiting for a moment while the woman typed slowly into her computer. It took an unusual amount of time for such a simple request.

"Holy shit," Abby said, throwing her hands in the air.

As Abby began to walk away, the woman said "He's ready for you" in such a monotone voice that Ryan cringed.

"Where is he?" Ryan asked.

"Are you kidding? Let's just go find him," Abby said. Ryan shook his head at himself and left with Abby.

The more they walked through the courthouse, the more they noticed that something was definitely wrong. Everyone who worked there acted like the receptionist they had just encountered. They all acted like they were hypnotized or drugged, performing their routine tasks like robots that were losing power.

"What the fuck is going on?" Ryan asked, proving Abby's earlier thought about him sounding a lot like her now. Not that it was a bad thing, and the edge that his personality had taken had given him the highest arrest record over the last couple months. A couple of the cops down at the station even referred to him as Super Cop. Lame, but it made Ryan feel good. And many of his coworkers were amazed with the changes. He was a fit guy before and a great detective, but lately, he seemed unstoppable. After surviving the events that happened in the winter, I guess anyone would seem destructible.

Getting to Alexander's room was odd too. The only ones alert were the hellhounds that greeted Ryan and Abby. The two guards at the door were just as dazed as the rest of the employees, if not a little more so.

"Can I enter?" Abby asked one of the guards. He looked back at Abby blankly. His eyes were so bloodshot that Abby wasn't even sure if he was able to see anymore.

Once it became obvious that he wasn't going to answer, Abby beckoned to Ryan to slip by them. Abby entered first and saw Alexander sitting on a small cot at the back of the cell. He was wearing an orange prison jumpsuit. His hair was a bit grown out and messy, and stubble was visible on his once-clean-shaven face. Although he was gaining power, he was still a pathetic shell of what he once was thanks to Abby. At least, for now.

"If it isn't my beloved sister," Alexander said. His sinister voice broke through the silence with a small evil laugh that made Ryan shiver.

Alexander looked at Ryan and stared him down. "I know what you want to do to me, and it's not very professional, Detective," Alexander said, laughing even harder as he invited himself into Ryan's head. "Looks like you're already being corrupted."

Ryan shut his eyes and grunted. "Go, I'll meet you outside," Abby said, gently pushing Ryan out the door.

Abby closed the door, locking herself in the holding cell with only herself, Alexander, and her dogs. She walked over and sat down in front of the bars separating her from her evil relative.

"You look like shit," she said as she made herself comfortable.

"Well, orange isn't our color," Alexander said, pulling himself onto the floor to closely look his sister in the eyes.

"Seems we both prefer black anyway," Abby said, agreeing.

Alexander looked at Abby with a most off-putting smile. "I've been in the room long enough for you to snoop around in my head. You know why I'm here. Do you know who's picking up where you left off?" Abby asked bluntly. As blunt as she was, she also wasn't dumb enough to expect a straight answer from him.

Alexander's laugh echoed in the room. Abby closed her eyes and used Alexander's favorite trick against him. He began violently punching himself in the head, attempting to fight off Abby's presence in there. Alexander slammed his arms against the bars.

"Get out!" he screamed. But it was useless. Abby had already completed her task. She opened her eyes and questioned him with her answers.

"You don't know who's doing this, but you're just enjoying the power that comes along with someone carrying out your evil will. It must drive you crazy to know that you can be replaced," Abby instigated. Alexander looked frustrated at Abby for being aware of how clueless he was about the situation too.

"But the girls, if you're not consuming them for power, then where are they?" Abby tried going back inside his head, but he was too guarded this time.

"Who says I'm not?" Alexander said, smiling as he calmed down and returned to his old tormenting self.

Abby got up to leave. Alexander wasn't being a very big help, and the hellhounds had kept him completely secure. There was no point for Abby to keep wasting time on him. Her focus had to be on whoever was free in Harmon and living out Alexander's plans.

"Do come back now," Alexander said, followed by his eerie laugh. It was obvious he knew more than he was letting on, but he was shutting off that memory somehow. Abby left and closed the door after petting her hounds. She noticed a used food tray outside the room labeled A. Smith. Abby grabbed the main dish off the tray and put it in a new trash bag she took off the janitor's cart.

Abby looked for Ryan in the building, but when she told him to meet her outside, he took advantage of the vague request and took off outdoors, away from the crazy. Abby left the courthouse fast, doing everything she could not to make eye contact with the creepy receptionist. Abby looked around and saw Ryan sitting against his car, waiting, still holding his head. He looked up to see Abby.

"Are you okay?" he asked her as he went in for a hug. These tender moments with Ryan were getting few and far between.

"I'm fine, but he's not going to be much of a help. You and the chief were right," Abby answered, accepting his embrace.

"What about the creepy vibe inside?" Ryan asked, looking at the courthouse building.

"That might have something to do with him. I'm not too sure yet," she replied.

Ryan's hand went inside Abby's coat as he didn't want to let her go just yet. "What's that?" he asked, noticing the bag she had under her coat.

"Oh, you're going to want to send this to the lab," she said, handing Ryan the bag. Ryan opened it and looked at the dirty dish from the courthouse.

"What are you expecting them to find?" he asked.

"I'm hoping I'm wrong, but it might be human," Abby said.

Ryan closed the bag quickly and tied it before putting it in the trunk. "Let's go drop this off now then, and we can fill the chief in afterward," he said, opening the car door for Abby. Abby got in and watched Ryan walk around the car, still looking at the courthouse with a look of suspicion. He got in the driver's side and quickly locked the door. Ryan drove back to the police station.

The lab facilities weren't too far from the station, which was one of the many reasons the city decided to keep that location for the station instead of rebuilding elsewhere.

"So you think the girls are dead?" Ryan asked.

Abby looked at Ryan, surprised by his blunt question. "I think it's likely that at least one of them is dead," Abby said, not sure how to answer. After finding Cassie alive, it was hard to imagine that two other girls may be new victims, especially since the man responsible was securely behind bars.

Ryan pulled up to their forensics lab. It was a small building with no windows. The yellow siding made it look like an eyesore even though it was important. "Wait here, I'll be right back," Ryan said. He grabbed the bag with Alexander's plate out of the trunk and rushed up to the building after slamming the trunk closed. Abby looked out of the car as Ryan flashed his badge at an overhead camera and the doors were unlocked for him. Abby waited while he was inside, which was for only a few moments. She put on the radio. Instead of hearing about multiple gang fights and nonstop violence, there were announcements about upcoming festivals and events for kids. There was regular news as well, like traffic and sports. Harmon had become a regular city again, and she understood why the police wanted to cover up these new problems in order to protect that.

Abby listened to the radio and looked around at all the traffic on the main road they just pulled off. They were running out of time to keep this quiet, and Abby worried that Harmon would go back to how it was. She was so distracted in her thoughts that Abby didn't even notice Ryan come out of the lab building. He opened the car door and startled Abby.

"Done. It shouldn't take too long. Let's go let the chief know what's happening," Ryan said while he started the car.

Back at the station, the news about one or both of the girls being most likely dead wasn't sitting well with the chief as he waited for the lab tests from the plate collected. Because of the number of phone calls from the station in such a short time, the lab put a special rush order for the results. Unfortunately, since Abby was almost certain the girls were dead, getting to them in the first twenty-four hours was no longer a priority.

Ryan went to a small table in the corner of the station just inside the door. An aged coffee percolator was almost done filling up. He grabbed three mugs from a small shelf above the table and poured himself, Abby, and Chief Doyle coffee. Abby sat down with Ryan by his desk while the chief went in his office to call the lab once again.

Ryan's desk was against the wall. It wasn't much bigger than the desks that some of the regular cops had. He didn't have much use for it though; he was always out on the field and took his paperwork home. It showed that he didn't use it much, and other people seemed to use it for storage. There were papers and boxes of supplies stacked on it.

Ryan and Abby waited at the station for a while longer until Chief Doyle finally came out of his office. He looked disappointed and told them that it would likely be hours until they heard back from the lab. He told them that they should just go home and wait for his call. Abby was more than happy to go back home. *Home*—a word that finally had a meaning to her. Abby had only been to her old apartment a few times after the events that took place that winter. She stayed with Ryan until she was clear to move into her new place. Abby was aware that Ryan was toying around with the idea of moving in with her. It wasn't something she was against, but giving up something as simple as living aboveground is hard for normal people—whatever normal is.

2

*A*s Abby was getting in the car, she bent down to fix her boot but then heard a voice shouting their names. Ryan rushed to greet the winded officer and conversed with him for a moment out of Abby's earshot

"The chief needs us!" Ryan shouted, looking back at Abby. Abby finished adjusting her boot and slammed the door. When they walked in, the chief had just gotten himself together in full uniform and was preparing to leave.

"You two are with me," Chief Doyle said, pointing at their confused faces. Ryan and Abby followed, waiting for an explanation, which they finally got once the trio were alone in the chief's car. "One of the missing girls was found," the chief said.

Ryan turned and looked at the chief from the passenger seat. "Is she injured? Can she talk? What was the description?" Ryan's questions overwhelmed Chief Doyle quickly.

"You know as much as I do. I just got the call, and we're headed to the hospital now," the chief said. The hospital and the memories Abby had there just came flowing back—memories of when she killed the giant freak that worked for Alexander and the brutal bloodbath created when the hellhounds devoured Alexander's men. The two familiar male voices faded away as Abby looked out the window at the city. She used to hate sitting in the back seat of a car when she was younger. It made her feel like a child or somehow inferior. It's odd what kind of hang-ups we had when we're younger.

The parking lot of the hospital was almost entirely clear. Each time Abby had ever gone past this hospital prior to last winter, it was always packed with cars and people; lately, the staff had it easy.

Abby followed Ryan and the chief into the hospital. Ryan looked back multiple times, making it obvious he was checking to see if Abby was still there. When they got up to the entrance, the doors slid open automatically. That was one of the many upgrades. The damage that was done just a couple months before was all repaired now; it looked like a brand-new hospital.

The chief went to receptionist to check in. Abby couldn't hear what they were saying, but the woman greeted him with a smile and seemed happy to help him, unlike that creepy receptionist at the courthouse. It still gave Abby shivers whenever she thought about it.

Ryan came over and stood with Abby. "I want to spend time with you tonight, somewhere special, after all this," he said softly in her ear. Abby smiled, still not sure what "all this" was going to be. The chief came back over and patted Ryan on the back with such force that he fell forward a tiny bit.

"Shall we?" he said, leading the way for Ryan and Abby to follow. They did follow, once again demonstrating their trust for Chief Doyle. When they got to the room, Abby waited by the door while the chief and Ryan did their jobs. A young girl was lying on the bed, conscious. It was hard for Abby to tell if her eyes were open or not because of the swelling on her face, but the girl was holding a stuffed animal and moving her hands a small bit to feel it.

"Hello, Elizabeth," Chief Doyle said as he approached the hospital bed holding the young girl, her shaking parents by her side. *Elizabeth. Liz,* Abby thought to herself. Her heart dropped. Another Liz affected by this animal. Abby felt guilty for almost giving up on this girl and believing she was dead. It seemed impossible that such a small, helpless girl could escape the amount of evil she was against.

Abby tried to listen as they spoke with the girl. Her description of the man who took her wasn't something Abby wanted to hear. Elizabeth told the chief in detail what he looked like. Abby looked at Ryan's face. He didn't seem as alarmed as her, so he hadn't made the connection of who it was yet.

Stephen, Abby thought to herself. Stephen was the last living member of Alexander's men. It didn't make sense because Abby knew he hated Alexander and hated working for him. He was only alive because Abby saw the good in him—good that was somehow now completely corrupted. The last Abby had heard, Stephen was a key witness in the upcoming trial but stopped checking in with the courts other than by e-mail. Abby quietly backed away from the door, unnoticed because their attention was on the victim.

Although she was tempted to borrow the chief's car, she knew how much it would be frowned upon after the last time she took off with a cruiser—for good reason, of course. Abby knew that she couldn't keep involving regular people in these kinds of things. Regular people die too easily.

Abby left by foot toward the courthouse, thinking that she may be able to think clearer and solve this quicker if she wasn't worried about the safety of whoever was with her. Both the hospital and the courthouse were near the middle of town, so it wasn't very far. And since it was finally decent weather, it wasn't a bad walk either—other than the thoughts and out-of-control emotions being triggered inside Abby.

She regretted not killing Alexander so much that she was beginning to hate herself more than anyone else. She wanted to use her evil abilities for good and try to make a pure, law-abiding decision by having him arrested to answer for his crimes. But is it good or evil to let such evil continue existing when you had the power to stop it? Abby's heart raced. She felt responsible once again, except now it wasn't just Alexander's future crimes she felt responsible for but Stephen's as well. How could someone change so drastically? Her mind raced with questions.

Even though Abby and Ryan had just been to the courthouse a few hours prior, it looked oddly different. It was the same structure, of course, but even though it was a sunny midafternoon, it seemed like the area was darker. Abby sensed that something horrible was going to happen or was already happening given the obvious look of evil. As soon as Abby got inside the door, she noticed an odd smell—a mixture of body odor and rot. She looked around and noticed the receptionist again. It was the same woman sitting there, only this time, she looked up from her desk and locked her eyes on Abby before Abby had even walked over to her desk.

Abby looked away and walked to the room Alexander was held in when she visited last. As she walked down the long hallway to the room, she noticed eyes on her. The eyes that were glazed over and dismissive last time she was there were now attentive and interested, like they had been expecting her to come. Abby rushed to the room to find it locked. A small window let her see the hellhounds were still on guard, but she couldn't see the corner cell and get a clear view of Alexander though.

Abby saw a man passing by, pushing a cart full of food trays for the prisoners held at the courthouse. "Excuse me, can you open the—" Abby wasn't able to finish before noticing the eerie presence; it was a man full of hatred—a man who gave her similar feelings she had toward Alexander.

"Stephen?" Abby said in shock. Without delay, Stephen grabbed something from his side and jumped at Abby. The halls were dark like the rest of the building, but Abby could see the shine from the blade Stephen was trying to stab her with. This wouldn't have happened if Abby wasn't so caught off guard.

Abby screamed as she fought off the attacker, trying not to lose her cool. Her screams echoed through the courthouse, catching the ears of her loyal dogs just inside the door she was closest to. The hellhounds burst out the room, knocking the heavy door onto the floor, and they crawled over it to get to their master even though their interest was mostly in eating her attacker.

The wall around the door crumbled, but the falling debris just bounced off the dogs' rough fur and didn't faze them. Abby watched from the ground as one of the dogs grabbed Stephen by the back of the neck and dragged him off her. His screams were muffled by blood filling his mouth. Abby froze, looking at her hounds ripping the flesh from someone again—someone she thought she had saved.

What else have I been wrong about? she thought, questioning herself and her previous actions. Her mind was spiraling. Abby's was so focused on her own thoughts and on the death happening right in front of her that she didn't notice the crowd of screwed-up court employees who were closing in behind her, and the most important thing that went unnoticed was the fact that Alexander was now left unguarded in an open room.

Once Abby calmed herself down, she looked around and realized Alexander was unguarded. She went to rush over to the room, but she was grabbed by multiple people. Her arms and legs were held by security men who were very clearly under some kind of influence. Abby struggled to get free, trying not to lose her cool and kill everyone in sight since they probably had no idea what they were doing. Abby yelled when the demented receptionist grabbed her long red hair. The woman screamed as Abby's hair flamed, causing immediate burns to the woman's hands.

"What's happening?" the woman screamed. "What are you guys doing to her?" The woman continued freaking out as she looked at Abby being attacked and held down by her coworkers. The severe pain from her burned hands had freed the woman's mind from the zombie-like state she was in. Abby struggled but continued to try calming herself down. It would have been easy for her to incinerate the whole crowd of people, but she knew they weren't bad.

The woman tugged at her coworkers to try and get them off Abby, but they didn't even notice her. "I don't know what to do!" the woman yelled, looking down at Abby. Just then, Abby's head was overpowered with evil. It was more intense and powerful now. Abby shut her eyes hard and hung her hand, trying to make the horrible feeling subside.

"He's coming. Hide!" Abby yelled at the woman. The woman looked around for a moment, clearly unsure of who and what

Abby was talking about. The woman was already in a panic and went to run down the hall before noticing the hellhounds eating what was left of Stephen. The woman screamed in terror as she ran the other way and ducked into a janitor closet. Abby could still see her peeking out, trying to watch what was going to happen, with her hands covering her mouth.

Abby looked away from the closet holding the woman and back at the door to see Alexander walking out his room. It was never the jail cell holding him, just the hellhounds, who were now too focused on finishing off Abby's attacker. His sinister smile had grown, and his look was now back to what it once was. His black hair shined with a hint of red, and his skin was as clear and pale as Abby's.

There stood her brother, the most magnificent display of evil she had ever seen. He smiled and laughed, but before he could speak, he was interrupted by the sound of glass smashing and men's voices. Ryan and the chief led a small number of officers who ran into the courthouse and down the hallway. Their work boots on the courthouse floor made the bland artwork on the walls shake.

The officers opened fire on Alexander without delay just as the hellhounds turned and noticed him. The bullets did nothing but melt as they approached Alexander. As the hounds jumped at him, Alexander vanished into the ground. The hounds fell to the floor, looking around. It was like he sunk into the ground or was sucked into it. All the workers who had their hands on Abby now let her go. The people seemed confused and disoriented. As soon as Alexander was gone, they were back to normal—a confused normal anyway.

Ryan walked over to the area of the floor where Alexander vanished. "Can you do that?" he asked Abby. He was still in shock from walking in on what just happened.

"I bloody hope not," Abby said, catching her breath.

"Let's get these people looked at!" commanded the chief. "Are you all right?" he asked.

"I'm fine. There's a woman hiding in that closet that probably needs help," Abby said, pointing to the door that was partly opened. The chief walked over and opened the door while Abby watched. The woman had her hands over her eyes and was rocking back and forth. The blood from her burned hands was leaking onto her face and clothing now. She was still screaming and crying as she rocked herself back and forth, probably trying to convince herself that what had just happened wasn't real. If only that were true. After all the employees were taken to the hospital, the courthouse was declared a crime scene.

"How are you?" Ryan asked, leaning against the wall beside Abby.

"I'm fine. How is everyone else?" she asked. Ryan looked over at the confused crowd.

"The receptionist thinks she's crazy from what she witnessed. Other than that, the rest of them remember coming to work the morning Alexander was transferred but nothing after that," Ryan said. He walked over and stood at the area where Alexander vanished beneath. He kept hitting the floor with his foot.

"I don't think it was a trick," Abby said. "At least not that part."

Ryan turned to her. "What do you mean?" he asked.

"I'm not sure. It just seemed like he expected me, and Stephen's life was just a sacrifice so he could escape," she tried to explain.

"I'm not sure if this is even possible, but each time I find out more about this guy, he just becomes worse and worse," Ryan said.

The three hellhounds sat near Abby. Stephen's blood was still soaking the fur around their mouths and dripping off their large fangs. The chief came back over to check on Abby before leaving to assemble a team to track Alexander down. His concern over Abby was confusing. She was expecting him to be very upset with her and the dogs for not being able to stop Alexander from escaping. He was such a good, understanding man. The hellhounds' eyes followed the chief as he walked away from their master.

Abby stayed with Ryan until he was ready to head back to the station. He remained professional, but she could tell he was a bit upset with her. Abby had a habit of dealing with things on her own since she was more durable, but Ryan didn't like those situations. He wanted to have an equal part in their professional and personal partnership.

"Do you want me to wait for you?" she asked.

"You can wait in the car. I'll be out in a minute," Ryan replied, handing the keys to her. Abby took the keys and left the courthouse. Unfortunately, Ryan's approval wasn't the most important thing on her mind right now. In fact, always having to do things by the book or by Ryan's standards was starting to get on Abby's nerves. Abby sat in the car thinking about where Alexander might be or what his plan was. And the question of how he influenced all the courthouse workers was tormenting her too.

Ryan got in the car and started driving without words. Hopefully there would be more answers at the station.

3

*T*he station was hectic. They drove up, and it was the busiest either one of them had ever seen it since winter. It had just happened an hour prior but word of Alexander's escape had already begun to fly. Now nothing was able to be kept quiet. As Ryan and Abby walked into the station, the atmosphere and personalities of everyone changed. Abby could feel glares in her direction even before she saw them. Some of the officers really hated her now. Most of their evil thoughts were still directed at Alexander, but they were blaming her for his escape. Abby didn't need people blaming her; she had been blaming herself since winter. After all, it was on her birthday that Alexander lost half his power and had to supplement it with much more evil endeavors that put the city of Harmon at risk. It's hard to feel good about anything when you feel bad for even being born.

The thoughts from the officers seeped into Abby's mind. *Why didn't she just kill him before? Did she let him escape? Is she working with her brother now?* The officers had lost all trust in her now. Abby wanted to be angry with them, but the rational side of her brain couldn't blame them. If she were in their shoes, she would be feeling the same way. Ryan wasn't as calm about things anymore though.

"Why'd you do it, huh?" an officer said as he approached Abby and grabbed her arm. The fat cop was clearly upset he had to put down his Danish and do some actual police work. His grip made Abby get a little angry.

"I didn't," she said, but there was no use. They had made up their minds.

"Take your hands off of her," Ryan said. His face was so close to the other officer's face that she could see goosebumps form on the officer's neck before he let her go. His eyes looked at Ryan's hand, which was placed on his gun in a threatening manner. They walked quickly to the chief's office, but they were stopped by another officer. He looked at Abby with such hatred.

"You evil little bitch," he said, raising his hand in an aggressive fashion. Abby thought the hellhounds that had followed her back from the courthouse were going to finalize their decision about her evil nature by ripping another cop apart in front of the entire station, but before they got the chance to even growl at the cop, Ryan blocked his punch with his left arm and hit him with his right fist so hard that the second cop didn't get up. Another cop attempted to grab Ryan, but he lifted him and tossed him like a sock monkey. The first cop who grabbed Abby made the mistake of joining the escalating fight, but Ryan was too far gone. He jumped on the officer and began beating his face over and over. Blood splattered and poured from his mouth and nose. His eyes were already swelling shut.

"Ryan!" Abby screamed, trying to get his attention off his rage. Other officers rushed over, but before they got there, an overwhelmingly loud gunshot was heard. Abby's ear rang a bit, and she put her hands up to cover them. Chief Doyle stood outside his office door, holding his gun in the air. A small amount of smoke blew away from the recently fired weapon. The chief looked at his officers with an expression of both anger and disappointment.

"At a time when we need to be working together, we're going to allow ourselves to fall apart? If all you're interested in doing is turning on each other, then go, get out of my station, and turn in your badge." Chief Doyle's words were professional but stern. He motioned for Abby and Ryan to come into his office. As they walked away, Abby looked back. Though they were abiding by their chief's order, they couldn't stop their thoughts and feelings, and Abby didn't need to read their minds to know what those glares still meant. Abby walked behind them into the office and shut the door.

"Sit," Chief Doyle said, pointing to a new leather couch in his office. "I got this when the city started thriving. I figured things had finally changed." He looked around his redone office. Now that the city actually had money, the officers had new weapons, and many of the cruisers had been replaced. It seemed even the police department got a little too comfortable with the newfound peace in the city.

"Sir, Abby didn't do—"

Ryan was cut off when Chief Doyle raised his hand. "Detective Finney, your behavior over the last couple months has been confusing, to say the least," the chief mentioned.

"I've gotten more arrests and criminals off the streets than any other cop. Should I *not* have done that, sir?" Ryan asked sarcastically.

"True, but you've also had more complaints of excessive force than any other cop, and that's not something we can continue to ignore, especially after the incident just now," the chief continued. "Considering what's happening, I can't afford to lose any officers in any way, including suspension. So I'm going to ask the both of you to leave for the rest of the night and come back in the morning when things have calmed down."

Ryan got up, visibly upset. "Sir, we need to start working now. We don't have time for this," Ryan said, making a valid point.

"And you can work, but not here. Not after the beating you just gave one of our own."

"But, sir—" Ryan attempted to cut in but was quickly shut up by the chief's sharp voice.

"I know he wasn't in the right, but I also have been witness to events proving this young lady can take care of herself," Boyle said, pointing to Abby. "There was no need for you to do that," the chief continued, shutting Ryan up. "Now I suggest you leave for the night like I said before you make things worse for yourself, Detective."

Ryan looked furious and stood in his place. "Come on," Abby whispered, trying to get Ryan to follow her without further incident. He listened but stomped past her, flinging the chief's door open. Ryan walked directly out of the station, knocking two officers out of his way with his broad shoulders. Abby followed, noticing that the hounds had already left, likely headed back underground to meet her there. Abby nodded at the chief and put her head down as she followed Ryan out of the station. She quickly glanced at the officer whom Ryan beat up. He was now sitting on a chair, and a female officer was tending to his badly wounded face.

"Ryan?" Abby said, rushing out to the car. Ryan was around the side of the building, punching the side of a cruiser.

"My behavior has been confusing? My whole fucking life is confusing. After what happened, he's surprised my behavior is confusing?" Abby let Ryan continue to rant and rage. This was something she was an expert in. After deciding he had dented the police car enough, he turned and walked to his car.

"Let's just go," he said, throwing a rock at the building. Abby looked down at his hands. He was so enraged that he didn't noticed the broken skin on his knuckles from hitting the car.

"Why don't we go to your place for a while? Maybe it will make you feel calmer being at home."

Ryan gave Abby a dirty look. There were a lot of those coming her way today. "Absolutely. Being surrounded by memories of my family that a current prison escapee killed would definitely help. Brilliant," he said, words dripping with sarcasm.

"Or you could just continue being a douche," Abby said, totally dismissing him as she slammed her door.

"Let's just go to our place," Ryan said. His calmer tone sounded very forced. Ryan started the car and drove. Abby wanted to act endeared by the fact that he saw her place as theirs, but she was still pissed off at his attitude.

"Whatever," she said, looking out the window, ignoring him. The drive there was quiet. The sun was going down, and it was beginning to get dark. The day went by so quickly today. Word of Alexander's escape must have made it to the public because there were very few people out on the streets.

Ryan parked on the side street, and they walked up to the tunnel. Even though there was some anger still in him, Ryan took Abby's hand as they walked through the tunnel so she wouldn't fall. They looked around like they always did before uncovering the ladder that led down to the second set of tunnels. The hounds were still lying in the tunnels, lounging. Now instead of growling, their signature noise was snoring. Abby and Ryan walked around them and took the second stairs down to her apartment.

Hecate was lying belly-up on the plush red chair Abby kept beside her bed. Abby sat down next to Hecate to take her boots off and gave her belly a rub. Ryan took his shoes off and walked over to the end of the room. He sat on the bed.

"I don't understand why all this rage is inside me. I don't know how to deal with it," Ryan said, trying to open up to Abby. Abby walked over and sat beside him.

"Can I look?" she asked, holding her hands out, about to touch each side of his head. He nodded, giving her permission. Abby touched his head. She could feel his rage, but there wasn't any obscene evil thoughts in his head—nothing new anyway. There was the typical want to kill Alexander, but that was the same for most people in Harmon. Abby recognized the random urge to be violent and the rage he was feeling. They were the same feelings she tried with years of counseling to solve, but it's always there.

Ryan groaned in relief as Abby shared the burden for a moment and took on some of the unwelcome feelings Ryan had been struggling with, even providing a moment of calm for him and making him feel better for a while. She cradled his head as he opened his eyes and came back with a bit more clarity. He grabbed her face and kissed her deeply before throwing her on the bed.

Ryan removed his clothes and crawled on top of Abby, grabbing the front of her jeans and undoing them before he ripped them down. Much like his attitude, his sexual habits had changed as well. His soft, gentle, but intense ways were now replaced with aggressive, rough, and impatient behavior. It was no longer lovemaking; it was rough, aggressive fucking.

Abby gave her body to him to do with as he pleased, giving him an opportunity to release whatever kinds of emotions he needed to. Ryan pulled Abby up and removed her shirt, revealing her large bare chest. Abby went to move into a different position, but Ryan pushed her down on her back. His head disappeared between her legs. His tongue made circles around the opening of her vagina before taking a shallow dip inside.

Abby's breathing became visibly heavier as his tongue got higher and higher toward the cluster of sensitive nerve endings that she could already feel her heart beating. Right before he made contact with her most sensitive part, he lifted his tongue. Abby bucked her hips, begging for more. He placed his lips around her clit and began sucking while his tongue played with the extremely sensitive flesh that was now sucked into his mouth.

"Don't stop," Abby panted as her eyes glowed because of the intense feelings. Abby moaned loudly as she grabbed the back of Ryan's head. Her legs wrapped around his neck while she humped his face to orgasm. Ryan rose up, his face dripping with Abby's moisture. He grabbed her and rolled her over with her ass in the air. Ryan brushed his rock-hard erection across Abby's ass before sinking himself balls deep inside her. He pounded Abby aggressively. Her yells were muffled by the pillow her face was being forced into. They were yells of joy; it was the perfect mixture of pain and pleasure for her.

Right before Ryan was about to finish, he pulled out and forced Abby to lie completely flat on her stomach. He lay over her, aligning himself up perfectly. Abby could feel his breath on the back of her neck. His hard, thick cock was resting between her ass checks. Abby knew what was coming next, so she took a deep breath as Ryan's cock entered her ass with one swift motion.

Abby bit down on a portion of the blanket they were on. He was so aggressive and didn't give her body time to adjust to the invasion anymore. The muscles in Abby's ass were so tight and sensitive that she felt every tiny movement inside her. As Ryan fucked her, he grabbed her long red hair and wrapped it around his hand to keep her from moving. It only took a few more pumps for Ryan to explode.

Abby could feel the involuntary movements his dick made as it pumped his warm load deep inside her ass. The postorgasmic sensitivity paired with how insanely tight her ass was made it hard for Ryan to pull out after he finished. He groaned as he did so and fell on the bed beside Abby. Abby got up and quickly went to the washroom to clean up. As she darted to the bathroom, she could feel his juices leaking out of her and down her legs—a feeling she loved. Because of how aggressive Ryan was getting, Abby now had to clean up a small amount of blood after each sexual encounter with him. To anyone else, that would be way over the line, but Abby didn't mind. She wanted to do anything to help Ryan deal with these unwanted violent urges he had.

Abby got in the shower and cleaned herself up. She let the hot water run down her body as she disappeared in thought. Although Abby may be able to deal with Ryan's new personality, she worried about his future with the Harmon police force and whether the chief would ever be able to trust the new him. He was still Ryan but was so much more unpredictable. Abby remembered what happened a few weeks prior. Ryan was so mad at one of the hellhounds for being in his way that he kicked it. The normal Ryan would never kick an animal even if it was an animal he couldn't hurt. After the hellhound realized what had happened, Abby had to stop it from eating Ryan. They accepted him and got used to him, but they also didn't take abuse from anyone anymore.

Abby shut off the water and grabbed a towel off the holder just outside the shower. She wrapped herself in it and got out. Abby stood at the sink and began to wipe down the fogged-up mirror with a small washcloth by the sink. She brushed her wet hair before putting it in one long braid to the side.

Abby was only away a few minutes, but when she got back to the room, she saw that Hecate had joined Ryan on the bed, and they were both passed out. She got dressed quietly. Abby wanted to let Ryan sleep as it was already late, and Abby was most productive at night. Her thoughts began to go back to Alexander and whether he would try and come there. He knew where she lived, but he also knew the hounds were there. It would depend on how desperate he was. Abby sat down on a chair in the small sitting room across the open-concept apartment.

"Oh shit," she said, feeling how tender her holes were from the thorough love session she just had. After thinking about it and weighing her options, Abby decided she would let Ryan sleep for the night and go out to try and find her brother on her own. She grabbed her boots and pulled them on. Hecate was watching closely. Abby walked back over to the bed. "Stay here, I'll be back," she said, petting Hecate on the head before leaving.

Abby climbed up to the second tunnel, trying to avoid waking up the hounds. *Maybe I should bring a couple,* Abby thought. Before she could say anything, two of the closest dogs got up and went to Abby. "I can't get anything past you guys, can I?" she said, petting the hellhounds behind the ears like they were regular dogs. Abby got up to the tunnel and saw the opening.

Usually light shined through, lighting up the tunnel, but it was the dark of night now, and even the moonlight was no help.

Abby walked along the ledge that was made for her while the dogs walked beside her, not worried or concerned of where they were stepping. Abby used the stairs to climb down the opening and to the car. She pulled out a small key chain from her pocket. On it was a key to Ryan's car; he had made it for her since they were basically living together. She got in the driver's side after letting the hounds in the back. Abby had started the car before realizing she had no idea where to start.

"The courthouse, right?" she asked, looking in the back seat at the glowing red eyes staring back at her. As much as Abby adored Ryan, spending time alone with her beasts was the most relaxed she'd been. She had been worried for so long about making sure Ryan was calm because of his changing attitude that she had forgotten to make sure she was calm. Ryan could lose his job over his aggression, but if Abby lost control, there would be loss of life.

Abby drove quickly to the courthouse. The caution tape that was put up a few hours ago was already falling down and blowing in the wind. The door was taped up with a Do Not Enter sticker over across it. The large glass windows around the door and the front of the buildings were boarded up, at least in places where the police had to smash in order to enter.

Abby took a small knife out from her thigh-high boot and cut the sticker off the door. She then stuck the same knife in the lock and was able to unlock the door within seconds. She walked in to find that the crime scene cleanup hadn't been very thorough. The building smelled horrible still, and as soon as Abby got near the room where Alexander was kept in, she noticed all the blood near the wall across from the door.

The dogs remained behind her until they approached the area. One of them, still dripping with blood, walked over to the scene and sniffed around, almost as if it recognized the area. Stephen's remains had been cleared, not that there was much left, but his blood still stained the floor. The sound of tearing flesh was not something Abby could ever get used to.

Abby walked into the room that held the jail cells. Alexander's cell looked normal, and he didn't cause any damage except on the lock itself. The lock to the cell had been melted off completely. As Abby looked closer, she could see that the bars around the lock showed signs of melting from being heated up as well. *So that's how you got out,* Abby thought to herself. *That's not as clever as I thought you would be.*

Alexander wasn't at full power yet, but with the help of Stephen, he was able to get close, even behind bars. Abby's head wandered; where would he be hiding this time? What could possibly be his plan now? All that was certain was that someone who should never be on the streets was now roaming free again. Once again, Abby's regret over not killing Alexander in the winter crept up on her and made her feel like shit.

Abby ran to the car with her hellhounds close behind. She got in after allowing the hounds to get in the back. "Now what?" she asked, looking at the glowing eyes that were in the dark back seat staring back at her. Abby didn't want to go home to Ryan without solving this problem for good. She wanted to solve this and then figure out why Ryan's personality was changing. She wondered if it could be Alexander. He was so deeply implanted in Stephen's head that he was able to bring him back to his evil side whenever he needed him.

She recalled the moments she and Ryan were separated during the winter's events. None of those encounters between Ryan and Alexander were long enough to affect his personality in this way. Abby tried to put aside her feelings and focus on the most important thing right now: finding Alexander. She decided she would check Alexander's old spots, except the tunnels obviously. The number of hellhounds still layering the hallways would make it impossible for Alexander to enter. Well, he could enter; leaving in one piece would be the problem. Townsquare wasn't far, but Abby didn't want to chance going on foot and having the hounds seen by any members of the regular public.

Abby drove to the side of the building and shut the car off. The hounds waited eagerly for her to exit the car and let them out. They followed so close that Abby kept feeling them touch the back of her legs. The building was still boarded up, but it was in the process of being completely redone outside and inside. New words were hung on the front of the building just above the entrance. "City Hall" could be seen in large blue letters. The building was known as Timesquare until two months ago. It got its nickname from the large clock on top of it. The clock was broken and was just for decoration for as long as Abby could remember. A building in Townsquare called Timesquare—it was obvious the city had stopped trying for a couple decades.

The large decorative clock had been removed during the remodel, so it looked so much better. The lower level of the building was still boarded up to keep any pests out, not that there were many issues since the city was much more peaceful over the past few months. Abby removed one of the boards from a lower window and climbed in. It turned out that she was the only pest they would have to deal with.

She looked back to assist the dogs, but they jumped in through the opening with no problem at all. The inside was still dark but felt much calmer. There was already new carpeting, and the walls were freshly painted. The smell of paint and floor cleaner were very noticeable. Abby moved from room to room, searching it for any sign of her evil brother. She knew deep down that if she didn't sense him there already, he probably wasn't there. But he was always so full of tricks. Abby took no chances, so she continued searching the rooms, hoping that there would be a clue to another place where he regularly hid.

She kept climbing stairs and going higher in the building, floor by floor, until she got to the door of the room she was held in by Alexander after that giant stalker freak kidnapped her in the winter. Abby never had anxiety until now, and she wanted to make everything that was causing it disappear. She opened the room; it was completely empty.

Fumes of fresh paint from the room flooded where she stood, and one of the hellhounds snorted the fumes and sneezed. The door had a label holder on it; the room was ready to become someone's office. Abby slowly walked into the space and stood in the middle of the room, looking around. Her memories of waking up in the bed that wasn't there anymore came flooding back, then the disgusting experience of finding the body of that poor girl in the very same bed just days later. There wasn't evil in the room now, but Abby's thoughts started getting evil, and she could feel her face getting so hot. Before she lost control, she noticed her loyal hellhounds were even beginning to back away from her. Abby shook her head and left the room quickly. She shut the door tightly behind her.

"That room shouldn't even exist anymore," she said, looking down at her hounds. Abby thought to herself, *All the terrible things that happened in that room and someone is just going to use it as an office like it's just some regular room. It doesn't seem natural.* Abby wanted to turn around and burn the room away, but she knew that would turn into her leveling the whole building.

"Well, he's not here. We better leave before I get us into trouble," Abby said to the dogs following her as she headed back downstairs. She felt anger and anxiety for not finding Alexander as easily as she was hoping to. He had killed so many people. The lone survivor of an entire family Alexander killed was close to her. She felt like she was letting Ryan down so hard and, by doing so, letting all his other victims down as well.

She didn't understand why Ryan didn't hate her, or maybe she wanted him to hate her as some form of punishment. She was willing to do anything to make Ryan happy and let him do anything as well. Perhaps that was why Abby was so submissive when it came to Ryan when she was so dominating to everyone else, because she felt like she owed him. Maybe that's why his attitude has changed so drastically, because Abby let him get away with so much.

Abby headed back to the car. When she got there, Ryan was standing beside it looking at her. He smiled, but his eyes looked angry and were focused on her. "You couldn't sleep either?" Abby asked quickly, hoping that would diffuse the tension. Ryan glared at her. He was completely dressed in black. His dark hair somehow looked even darker, and his skin was paler than it had ever been. He still looked like Ryan—just a very dark version.

Abby looked at Ryan, and she looked into his head briefly so he wouldn't know. She didn't like having to snoop around, but he wasn't as open lately. His hatred for Alexander was felt quickly. It was understandable but growing much too fast. The gore and violence he kept thinking about raining down upon Alexander was nothing like the thoughts he had before. His thoughts were very dark, and he was becoming very unpredictable.

"Are you feeling okay?" Abby asked, trying to act normal around this new Ryan.

"I just missed you when I woke up," he said without breaking eye contact.

"I haven't been gone more than an hour," Abby said. She walked to the side of the car where he was standing and opened the door beside him to the back seat. The hellhounds got in, and Abby shut the door. She felt Ryan running his fingers along her shoulder. Abby went to walk around to the other side of the car. She didn't notice Ryan following her. She had her back turned to him as she went to open the door, but he pushed it shut.

Before she could turn around and ask what he was doing, his hands were already reaching around her, tugging at her jeans. Ryan was holding Abby tightly between the car and his body. She could feel his breath on her neck as his hands wandered. Ryan grabbed her pants and roughly tugged them down just enough to reveal both her ass cheeks. Abby had just been inside his head and had no idea he was even thinking about doing this. She knew this wasn't the time and definitely not the place for this, but her guilt made her submit herself to him whenever he wanted her. If there was something she could do to create pleasure in his life, she was more than happy to do it.

One of Ryan's arms remained wrapped around her, holding her in place against the car while his other arm disappeared between her cheeks. Abby began to shake as Ryan stroked her from her clit to the opening of her ass. Abby gasped, unprepared when he pushed his finger inside her tiny anal opening. It was so tight and still so sore after the pounding from earlier.

Abby heard Ryan's pants unzip, and she was pushed against the car even harder. Without turning around, she knew what was about to happen. Abby put her arms on the car to hold on and closed her eyes. She could feel Ryan's hard flesh between her cheeks searching for an opening. The cold night air gave her exposed ass and hips goosebumps. Without warning, Ryan thrusted deep into Abby. She groaned, trying not to scream. Before, he would always give her body time to adjust; now he just went for it like a wild animal and took what he wanted.

Abby's legs gave out after the quick intrusion, but her legs were no longer needed because of how hard she was pinned against the car now. It was only a few minutes of being fucked relentlessly before she felt him finish. As soon as he was done, he pulled out roughly, this time making himself yell. Abby was still leaning against the car and getting the feeling back in her legs. Ryan zipped his pants and opened Abby's door. She fell into the car, and Ryan walked around to the driver's side. "I told you I missed you," he said as he started the car.

During Abby and Ryan's activity, the hellhounds had fallen asleep in the back. They were already used to chaos. Abby looked around, confused. Ryan was definitely not himself, and even though she was submitting to it, she wasn't sure if he was even noticing the changes. His primal urges were so much stronger, and now he would just do whatever he wanted. It happened in public so often now. It was as if he couldn't control his urges anymore.

Abby cleared her throat. "Where are we going?" she asked.

"The chief found something," Ryan answered. As soon as he answered, Abby noticed they were on their way to the station. As Abby sat there, she didn't engage Ryan in much more conversation. Although Abby healed faster than average people, she was still sore from what Ryan kept doing with her body. The previous Ryan was always so worried about her comfort, and now Abby was beginning to wonder who this was.

4

*T*he police station looked odd. Ryan and Abby didn't noticed as they drove up because their focus was on other things. The station had just been redone, but it looked like it aged somehow. The inside looked dark, even for nighttime. They both got out of the car and looked at the building. Abby looked at Ryan and was about to comment on it, but he walked inside without hesitation. *Okay,* Abby thought to herself. He was acting like he was the one who was unstoppable.

Abby waited for a moment. Not only was he acting more like her, but he was also acting like Alexander. Once again, she wondered if Alexander was doing something to Ryan's mind. She walked into the police station with the hellhounds behind her and joined Ryan as he stood looking around. All the police officers had their hands on their desks and were facing away from them. Abby noticed the door didn't close, and as she closed it, something very odd happened. Every single officer looked up at them at the exact same moment. It was as if their movement was choreographed.

Abby's senses came back after Ryan had weakened them for a moment. An evil was in that building. But it wasn't the officers. When Abby tried to search around in their thoughts, it was like they were blank canvases, just like the people in the courthouse.

"We need to leave," Abby said.

Ryan looked back at her. "But I—"

Abby cut him off. "No, now," she said as she turned around and ran with her dogs at her side. The sound of Ryan's shoes hitting the ground rapidly behind them reassured her that he was following close behind. She got in the car, and the dogs jumped into the back. Abby punched the dashboard repeatedly. Ryan opened the door and slammed it as he got in.

"What's going on?" he asked, sounding winded.

"He's there. They called you because they caught him," Abby tried explaining. Ryan looked extremely confused.

"Alexander? Isn't that a good thing?"

Abby shook her head, remembering how Alexander had influenced the people at the courthouse. "Once he's got his strength back, he'll want to build an army again," she said. Ryan looked shocked, then fear rolled over his face finally.

"And these men are already armed and trained, not some street thugs who are easily corrupted," he added. Abby nodded in agreement. "What should we do? Both the cops and Alexander know where you live now."

"Let's go there. I need to grab Hecate and a few things before they do whatever he makes them do." Abby looked in the back seat at the hounds. She grabbed one of them by the face and whispered to it. "And you're going to have to tell your buddies to vacate the tunnels for a while."

Abby ran through the tunnels and went down to her place as fast as she could. Ryan ran fast enough but barely kept up. They made it there before anyone else had gotten to it. The hounds that were with them stayed on the second level and joined their fellow hellhounds scattered throughout the halls.

Abby rushed into her living space. The bed was still messed up from when Ryan had been sleeping. Abby kept her boots and a small leather coat on while she entered. She grabbed a dark-red backpack from a hook on the wall and began grabbing some things she needed—a couple of tank tops, some photos, a switchblade, and some other things.

"Is there anything else we can't replace? It seems like fire destroys a lot of things lately," Ryan said. Abby could tell he was attempting to lighten the mood, but she didn't have time to respond. Plus, thinking about the one place she actually enjoyed being destroyed wasn't a happy thought at all, and she was trying to keep happy thoughts in her head so she wouldn't start burning people alive.

As soon as she was done grabbing personal items, she went to her bed and grabbed Hecate. Abby wrapped her in a small blanket that she got from the drawer of her nightstand. She put Hecate gently in the bag too, keeping a portion of it open for air. Abby put the bag on her back and looked back at Ryan, who was still standing in the doorway keeping a lookout.

"I guess we better go," Ryan said. Abby walked to the door. She wasn't happy about leaving her new home but hoped she would be able to return to it soon. They climbed back up to the middle level. The hounds had already taken Abby's advice and vanished from the tunnels for the time being. Abby's heart dropped when she saw the bare tunnels. She was unsure when she would be reunited with her beasts. Ryan pulled on her arm to rush her along; this wasn't a time to mourn.

Abby and Ryan rushed up to the surface. They got to the top tunnels and finally stopped running. Ryan bent over, completely out of breath. The opening at the end of the tunnel showed a bit of dull light coming through. It was very early morning finally. Just as they were about to walk at a normal pace back to the car and figure out what was next, Abby heard a huge bang. It came from the opening above them—the tunnel Alexander used on the far side of the Townsquare grounds. The banging continued.

"Listen," Ryan said. The voice of Chief Doyle could be heard ordering his men to unseal the opening that Alexander regularly used in the winter. Chief Doyle had just ordered it permanently sealed three months ago; the order came directly from him. The sound of stomping boots and all the men speaking echoed through the tunnels. It sounded like most, if not all, the cops of Harmon were there. Abby and Ryan listened for a moment and heard the chief order half of the officers to go around to the tunnel opening by the river, which Abby and Ryan were about to use in order to exit the tunnels.

"I thought we had more time," Abby said, looking back at Ryan. Abby and Ryan ran as fast as they could back to the car. Just as they got to the opening, they saw the car. Two officers were standing at his car. They looked like they were posted in that location in case Abby and Ryan returned. As soon as the officers spotted the couple, they pointed their weapons at them without hesitation and prepared to fire. Abby's eyes glowed immediately, and her red hair flamed and blew with the wind. She was so on edge lately that it didn't take much to set her off anymore.

The weapons the officers were holding quickly melted into liquid that hardened on the ground. Ryan ran toward them while they were distracted by Abby's strange, forceful anger. Ryan surprised one of them out of his terror by punching him in the face. He fell on the ground completely knocked out. Abby got over to where Ryan was, but the second officer saw what Ryan had done to his partner and grabbed Abby by the neck. Hecate poked her head out of the backpack to see why she was being thrown around so much. Abby's skin glowed, and the officer's hand began steaming, which forced him to let go of her. Abby dropped to her knees and coughed. He had grabbed her neck with so much force. When she looked up, she saw Ryan looking at the officer's hand. His palms looked like fucked-up hamburger meat; the burns were so severe. Abby picked herself up with Ryan's help.

"We have to go now," he said.

"No," she replied, still catching her breath. "You saw them. They were going to shoot us with no questions asked. You heard the chief too. They aren't themselves right now," Abby pleaded.

Ryan nodded in agreement. "But what do you suggest? We can't just kill them. They aren't bad people. Unless killing them would weaken Alexander," Ryan said.

Abby was shocked that his mind would even think of killing his coworkers, especially the chief. Instead of getting distracted and asking questions, Abby looked past his odd statement. "No, they're underground. I simply suggest we keep them there while we fix this," Abby said.

Abby went back into the tunnel as quietly as possible using the stairs that were recently build. Abby and Ryan got to the hole with the small ladder that led to the second level of tunnels. It was open, and the police had already made it down to Abby's place. Ryan joined Abby in the tunnel and grabbed the large stone cover and placed it over the hole. Then they rolled other large rocks over to cover the hole and give it more weight just to make sure they couldn't get out.

"I can't believe this. Out of all the crazy shit that's happened, I can't believe this. I've always looked up to the chief. Ever since my parents ..." Ryan's thought process drifted off as he got a bit emotional, and he started clenching his fists.

"It's okay. That's not the chief down there. That's Alexander playing with his head," Abby said. She finished dragging the last large rock she could find to cover the hole. She dusted herself off as she stood up.

"That should do it," she said. She grabbed her backpack again, making sure Hecate was still in there. She noticed Ryan had a serious look on his face.

"Ryan?" Abby said, edging him to walk on.

"Alexander. If he was able to manipulate every single officer in Harmon, you don't think he's still at the station, do you?" he asked. Abby looked at him funny.

"Of course not, but we can start there now that the cops won't be just waiting there and ready to kill us," she said, leading him out of the tunnel. As they left, they heard one of the trapped cops banging on the opening. Ryan looked back with sympathy in his eyes for his fellow officer now that they were aware of being trapped underground. Abby looked confused at Ryan; he mentioned killing them, but he still cared about this. It didn't make sense.

"It's okay, they're safe from whatever is going to happen up here," Abby said, reassuring Ryan.

Ryan got outside the tunnel first and walked toward his car. He turned around and gasped. Abby followed his line of sight. The number of cop cars that were left unattended now confirmed Ryan's theory that every single cop in Harmon was now trapped belowground.

"We need to get to the station," Ryan said with worry. They rushed to the car and drove there as quickly as possible with very few words. Abby's head was filled with thoughts, mostly thoughts about how she should have killed Alexander before. Abby could sense the presence of Ryan's evil thoughts. Although she was worried about the change in his personality, she was used to sensing everyone's evil thoughts when it came to Alexander. Everyone in town wanted him dead, but no one had the power to do it. Abby did, once. But now Abby was worried that he was going to become much more powerful than her, making it impossible to take him down single-handedly.

The police station looked completely deserted. Ryan pulled in and parked right out front—it wasn't hard to find a parking spot now. Abby kept her bag and Hecate in the car while they went in to check things out. They got inside the police station. It was completely empty. The officers' chairs were tipped over, like they all left in a hurry. Abby walked to the back and checked the lock, not that she believed Alexander would still be in there voluntarily. This time, instead of just melting the lock, the bars on that whole side of the cell had been melted down. There wasn't any need for it; this was nothing but a demonstration of power or anger. Either way, this wasn't good news.

Ryan walked into the room after clearing the rest of the station. "We're alone here, it seems," he said before looking around. He stood there for a moment and took in the sight until his eyes stopped at a far corner.

"What's that?" he asked, walking toward it. Abby quickly redirected her attention to where Ryan was looking. A small pile of bones were left in the corner of the cell.

"Could that be the remains of the girl?" Ryan asked with a disgusted look on his face. Abby walked over to the bones and squatted to look closer.

"They look human, so probably," she said. Ryan gagged and walked out the room. Abby gave him a moment before she joined him. Ryan was pacing back and forth and looked flustered.

"We have to find that asshole!" he shouted.

"I know. I'm also hoping he finds us and makes things a bit easier," Abby added. Ryan went into the chief's office and looked in his computer.

"There are no e-mails or memos about them storming your place. It was just done," Ryan said, trying to find any trace of orders that would make sense of the police force's actions. "Let's get out of here," he said as he walked past Abby and out of the station. Abby followed and got in the car with Ryan. She looked in the back to see Hecate sleeping in her bag. Her paws covered her eyes, and her little fangs hung out of her mouth.

Ryan and Abby sat in the car for a moment and looked around. It was completely light out now. People were beginning to come out of their homes and start their day, but this time, people went to their cars with haste. The blinds to everyone's houses were all pulled down, and people were starting to live in fear again. It wasn't as bad as last winter yet since people were still leaving their houses, but if Alexander remained free, then the city of Harmon would end up like it was before, if not worse.

Ryan started the car and began driving. "I don't know where to go. Everyone I trust is either in this car or trapped in the tunnels," Ryan said.

"Let's go to your place. We can gather our thoughts and maybe come up with something there," Abby suggested. Ryan agreed after thinking about it for a short moment. It wasn't a great idea, but it was the best one they had at the moment.

C H A P T E R

5

$\mathcal{R}$yan pulled into the parking lot attached to their old apartment building. It still looked the same despite their useless superintendent always promising to repave the terrible lot. He promised a lot of things he never came through on. Despite that, the older people who lived in the building attempted to make it look nice again when spring came by putting out small ornaments and planting flowers around the exterior. It didn't add anything to the aged building; all it did was attract bees.

Abby picked up the bag from the back seat, startling Hecate out of her sleep. They walked into the building to his door. There was no one in the halls at all. Before entering Ryan's apartment, Abby paused for a moment and looked at the door to her old apartment. So many memories in that place, but the bad ones easily replaced the good ones, and she was grateful to be out of there. The smell of weed now leaked out of her old apartment, and a weird goofy laugh could be faintly heard.

"At least the new guy is making good memories," Abby said when the smell of weed got very intense.

"It's legal now. Otherwise I would be busting his ass for that smelly shit," Ryan said. He obviously didn't like the new neighbor. Ryan unlocked the door, and Abby walked in behind him. She looked around to make sure there were no surprises and then set her bag down on the couch. Hecate poked her head out of the bag, then curled up, got comfortable, and continued sleeping.

Ryan went to the kitchen, obviously still upset about the situation they had found themselves in, which was understandable; he'd been dealing with things no ordinary human should ever have to deal with. Abby heard him switching on his coffee maker and banging two mugs on the counter.

"I can't believe I am about to sit here and drink coffee when all the officers of Harmon are trapped underground," Ryan said softly to himself. Abby didn't reply to any of his mumblings and just waited for him to come out and sit down. She looked around his place. It looked the same except for the dust buildup that came from him spending most of his time at her place. Ryan walked out of the kitchen and placed the two mugs on the long coffee table in front of them. He sat down, visibly upset.

"What would you rather be doing? We'll go start there," Abby asked, wanting to do anything at all to make things a little bit better.

"What would I rather? I would rather have to deal with none of this, but you let him live!" Ryan snapped to Abby's surprise. Hecate woke up, her tiny eyes glowing, and hissed at Ryan. She calmed back down to a mellow state when Abby started stroking her fur. Abby's temper told her to yell back violently at Ryan, but her brain reminded her that he wasn't wrong and retaliation would get her no victory here. She was also worried about getting angry at all with how quickly she was able to change and hurt those cops by Ryan's car earlier. He was acting like a complete dick, absolutely, but his words still were not wrong.

Abby didn't answer but kept petting Hecate. She reached over and grabbed her mug. Ryan looked at a family photo on a small end table and then down at his shoes.

"I'm sorry. I didn't mean that," Ryan said, hoping to smooth things over.

"You did, and you're right. I've been regretting it for a while now," Abby said.

"No, it's me," said Ryan. "I haven't been able to keep my temper in check lately."

Abby took a drink of her coffee—two creams, no sugar. At least he still remembered the small things. Ryan got up and was banging around in the kitchen again. He came back with a small bowl full of milk and set it on the table in front of them.

"I never offered her a drink," he said, trying to be less infuriating.

Hecate looked at the dish. She finally got up after deciding it was worth it. She walked over and started licking it up fast. Ryan went into the bathroom, and by the time he was back, the milk was gone. Hecate flopped down on her side and stretched out along the table before going back to sleep in that spot.

"Where do you think the hounds are?" Ryan asked randomly.

Abby looked away with a small look of sadness. "I have no idea," Abby answered honestly. She hoped she would see them again soon. "I just hope Alexander doesn't let the cops out until they're back to normal."

"Me too," Ryan said in agreement. "Do you really think those were the remains of the missing girl?" he asked like he wasn't the detective in the room. Abby shrugged, unsure of what her answer should be. The one girl who got away was still in the hospital, and police were posted at her door in case someone tried to come back to finish the job. The odd thing now was that the two cops posted at her door were likely the only two cops in their right minds right now. Ryan's frustration grew stronger with each passing minute.

"The lab should be open. I'm making a call," Ryan said before jumping up and going out on his balcony. The green curtain blew in the wind while Ryan talked on the phone with the door to the apartment open. Abby gulped down half of her coffee before he came back in, looking depressed.

"You were right. The DNA on the plates matched the girl that was being held with Elizabeth. The bones were probably leftovers he was storing," Ryan explained. Abby cringed at the term *leftovers* when describing a human being.

"We either find him fast or things are about to get a whole lot worse," Abby said, feeling her skin getting hot again. She focused on her breathing and tried to force her body into a relaxed state. Even though she completely hated anger management, she still occasionally utilized some of the techniques she was taught to try and calm down when things got out of control. Just as she was calming down, the annoying bass-playing neighbor that Ryan had mentioned started playing so loud. Abby held her head.

"We're not going to be able to stay here much longer anyway, but I'll tell him to keep it down," Ryan said as he left and knocked loudly on the door across the hall. The knocks were so loud you could tell he was a cop. Abby walked to the door Ryan had left open and waited to see if the new neighbor was going to open his door. Coughing and choking broke the silence on the other side of the door.

"Just a minute," said a male's voice straining to talk. Stumbling footsteps could be heard as he got to the door, unlocking uncountable locks. The door flung open. "What's up?" the voice said. Abby couldn't see his face as he was standing in darkness just inside the door. Smoke leaked out of the open door and filled the hall with even more weed aroma.

"Listen, I've been really cool so far about all this noise, but you know your neighbor is a cop, and you still keep doing it. It's just disrespectful now," Ryan said, beginning to get confrontational.

"Why don't you come on in, have a beer, and get disrespected some more?" The neighbor laughed in a mocking tone. Abby sensed something off about him, not in a negative way. But there was a draw to him that she couldn't fight.

"Is that an invitation? Can I join?" Abby said as she walked over to the door and was finally able to see his face. He was surprisingly handsome, but his good looks didn't match his less-than-acceptable hygiene. He had long blond hair that was tied back in a ponytail, and even though it looked like it needed washing, it shined with a beautiful golden tone. His skin glowed with a golden tone too, and his smile was perfect.

"Of course," he replied, looking intrigued at Abby. Abby noticed him look at her in the same way, almost like he knew she had a secret. His bright blue eyes followed her as she entered her old apartment with Ryan following right behind her.

"Did you even get his name?" Abby asked Ryan quietly.

"No, he didn't," replied the neighbor, who overheard. "I'm not up to his standards to speak to. I'm Joe," he said, sticking his hand out.

Abby shook his hand and asked, "Just Joe?"

Joe smiled. "Yes, just Joe. When you're passed around in the system so long, you get so many names that they really don't matter anymore." Joe walked around a coffee table to a large sofa that was facing a huge, old rear-projection TV.

"Please sit," he said, pointing to some cheap foldout chairs that were upright.

"How are they set out already?" Ryan asked. Abby looked confused.

"What do you mean?" Joe asked.

"There are three more chairs folded in the corner, but two of them were already set up like you were expecting two guests," Ryan accused.

Joe laughed and clapped. "Did you say you were a cop or a detective?" Joe asked, finding Ryan's accusing tone amusing.

"I'm both," Ryan said, leaning forward, looking at Joe's face. Joe got up and went directly in front of Ryan. He leaned down and stared in his eyes. Ryan looked at him with caution.

"You're really changing, aren't you, little guy?" Joe asked. Ryan was much taller and more built than average, but Joe was above average in every way. He didn't look like the type to work out, yet his biceps were massive. Ryan began breathing heavily.

"Move away from me," Ryan ordered.

"Oh yes, you're changing all right," Joe said as he skipped back over to his spot on the couch. For a man who looked to be about thirty-five, he was definitely childish. *Who is this guy?* Abby thought to herself. It was odd that Ryan didn't respond when his behavior was pointed out yet again. They sat in silence awkwardly for a moment, and Abby looked around her old place. Right beside where Joe was sitting, there was a huge bong, and pipes were displayed all over. Ryan clearly didn't like his new neighbor, but Joe seemed to have more concern for him.

When he looked into Ryan's eyes, Abby felt a similar feeling, like he was trying to look inside her head. "Put that down!" Ryan yelled. Joe was holding his bong and was about to light it.

"My house, my rules," he said as he flicked his lighter and inhaled the smoke deeply.

"So where are you from Joe?" Abby asked.

"Now that is a confusing story," he said while he coughed out some of the smoke. Small scratches alerted the three to Joe's closed door. Ryan got up and opened it. It was Hecate. Abby had left the door to Ryan's apartment partly open in case she wanted to follow them. Ryan let her in, and she walked right over to Abby and stood by her feet. Joe smiled at the tiny cat, who looked around the apartment so intelligently. Instead of sitting back down, Ryan stood by Joe's door.

"I'm going to get some air on my balcony. I can't stand the smell in here," Ryan said rudely as he left, pulling the door closed behind him.

"Does your boyfriend often leave you alone with strange men?" Joe asked jokingly.

"Oh, good, you already know you're strange," Abby joked. Joe laughed harder than Abby was expecting. His laugh turned into a cough. Abby waited until he was done choking.

"So who are you really?" Joe asked in a raspy voice.

"What do you mean?" Abby said defensively.

"There's something you're holding back," Joe said as he got a bit closer to her. Abby pushed him, and the stoner fell back onto his old couch.

"We just met. I'm sure there's a lot we're both holding back," Abby replied, trying to be as vague as possible with the familiar stranger.

"I get that, but does it feel like we just met to you?" Joe asked. Abby paused for a moment.

"Actually, no, it feels like I've known you for ages," Abby said. Hecate lay down at Abby's feet.

"At least one of you is comfortable here," Joe laughed again, looking down at the small black cat. Abby leaned down and petted Hecate.

"Actually, I used to live here," she said, finally opening up to the idea of a conversation with someone new.

"Oh, so you're the Abby that this belongs to then," said Joe, walking over to a small dresser and opening it. "Here," he said with his hand out. Abby opened her hand and looked at what was placed in it. It was her old name tag from Duffy's bar. She hadn't seen it since her last shift. Liz had a hell of a time getting Abby to wear her name tag because Abby hated when customers came up to her using her name. Abby looked down at the name tag, reminiscing for a moment.

"There are a lot of rumors about what happened to that bar across the street," Joe added.

Abby took a moment to answer because she was looking at her tag and thinking about last winter. "Whichever rumor sounds the craziest is probably true," she said. Abby put the tag in the pocket of her jeans.

"You can tell me about it. I mean, even if you don't trust me to keep quiet, who's going to believe an unemployed stoner?" Joe joked.

He has a point, Abby thought to herself.

Joe looked over at the TV, which was directly in front of the couch he was on. Reports about the missing police were already out. Abby glanced at the TV, trying not to make her interest known. The police cars had been found, but the officers were all still considered missing. Lucky for them, the general public were still too scared to go near the tunnels. The evil events that happened last winter had been leaked, and it was beginning to be like a game of telephone.

The story, which was already unbelievable, began to get even crazier. The last rumor Abby heard was that all of Alexander's furniture was made from human bone. Although Abby could totally see him doing that, it wasn't true. But everyone liked a good scary story, it seemed.

Abby sat back, wondering how long it would take for someone to get the balls and check the tunnels. The cops would be freed and would begin looking for them again as soon as they got out. Joe grabbed the remote off the old coffee table and turned off the TV, almost like he knew it was causing Abby torment.

The atmosphere around Joe was totally different from anyone else in her life. Abby felt comfortable, almost like they were the same. Not that Abby was a stoner—keeping her head clear was the only thing that kept herself and everyone else around her safe. It just felt like they were supposed to meet.

"So where did you move here from?" Abby asked Joe.

"I'm from all over like I said. I don't stay in one place too long," he answered. Abby smiled slightly.

"Are you on the run or something?" she joked. Joe looked at her with a grin.

"Something like that, I guess," he replied. He grabbed the bong beside him and a small round container from inside a tiny drawer in the end table and began to put more weed in it. Once he was done, he lit it. Abby watched him expel a huge cloud of smoke and begin coughing. During his coughing fit, Abby noticed something very strange. When she looked into his head, the more he smoked weed, the more clouded and blocked it was. The more he smoked, the more he was protected from her intrusion into his head.

Joe took another hit from his bong, and Abby looked around again. In the corner behind him was a sword neither she nor Ryan noticed. It was the brightest gold she'd ever seen. It definitely didn't match the other dull fixtures in there. On the handle was a lightning bolt.

"That's really beautiful," Abby said, pointing to the weapon.

"Oh, thank you," he said, turning around and grabbing it.

"Can I see it?" Abby asked.

"No," he said firmly. Odd. That answer didn't match his personality. "Sorry, it was a gift only meant for me," he said, trying to explain. Abby smiled. Finally, someone as weird as she was.

"So where did you move to?" Joe asked, changing the subject. Abby wasn't sure how to answer that. She couldn't just say that she moved underground.

"It's a pretty remote place," she answered. Joe laughed.

"We're both so vague and full of secrets, it seems," he joked. It may have been a joke to him but Abby was feeling the similarities between them already.

"What kind of cat is she?" Joe asked, looking down at Hecate by Abby's feet.

"Just a plain black cat," Abby said, leaning down and petting her on the head.

Joe laughed. "If you say so." He was such an odd guy; he hinted like he knew things without actually saying it. Abby was growing more intrigued and amused by him.

"You would have liked Liz. She would have brought you things from across the street," Abby said, randomly thinking about the many times Liz cooked up too much food over at Duffy's and brought it over to the older people in the apartment building. Joe put his bong down to listen.

"There are rumors that say she died in the fire, and others that say it was at the hospital," Joe said. Immediately he shook his head, disappointed in himself for bringing up Liz's death so easily.

"It was at the hospital," Abby continued. "There are not many genuinely good people left in the world, and there's one less now that she's gone."

Joe paused for a moment before speaking. "You seem like a good person," he said.

The sentence broke the sadness for Abby, and she smiled. "If you knew what I came from, you would understand why that is so funny and impossible," Abby said. Could someone who was literally born out of evil be considered a good person? Wouldn't that go against their own DNA?

Joe took yet another hit from his bong before speaking. "It's not about where you're from, it's about where you're going and what you do," Joe said, trying to hold in another coughing fit. Such wisdom coming from someone who looked like he hadn't been sober in years.

Just as Abby was about to open up to her new friend about who and what she really was, Ryan busted back into Joe's place.

"I just got a call from the hospital. One of my rookies had me listed as his emergency contact," Ryan announced, motioning for Abby to follow.

"Sorry," Abby said, picking up Hecate and hurrying toward the door.

"See you soon, Ms. Briggs," Joe yelled as they were leaving. Abby went across the hall into Ryan's place and grabbed her bag, securing Hecate inside it again before leaving. It took her until they got to the car to notice that Joe had called her Ms. Briggs even though she never told him her last name. *Who are you?* she thought to herself again while she looked back at the building.

Ryan drove quickly to the hospital but didn't want to attract more attention by turning on his siren. The streets only had people on them who had to be there—a few construction workers, mail couriers, and taxi drivers. There were barely any other cars on the road in midday.

Abby looked out the window as they drove. The parks that were full of kids just days before were now bare again. Small businesses that had reopened chose to stay closed again. TVs in shop windows were warning people to stay indoors. Reports of Alexander's escape and the missing police officers were everywhere. One headline read, "The devil is loose, and our officers have vanished." Normally, when breaking news hit, pedestrians would stop at the windows and watch the TVs for information, but this time, people were too busy getting home and locking their doors. All the progress that the city of Harmon had made these last few months was undone so quickly. Abby had never felt like a bigger failure.

The hospital parking lot had more cars than before. "I hope this is just for visitation," Ryan said. Abby nodded her head and agreed—one of the alternatives was that violent crimes drastically went up again. Ryan rushed to the doors of the hospital and went in to speak with the receptionist. Abby looked at the waiting area; it was full of people—from small injuries to head trauma. Some people were lying in corners with bags and luggage. There were entire families there who looked defeated and depressed. Ryan came behind her after finishing up at the reception.

"What happened here?" Abby asked. She didn't want to look inside the mind of a head trauma victim and cause any more damage.

"They were transferred here from the town over because the hospital there was destroyed. Apparently, Harmon is in the eye of a storm," Ryan answered. Abby looked around and out the glass doors. It was dull outside but still calm.

"There's a hurricane?" Abby yelled. Ryan looked into the waiting room at all the people and quickly looked away.

"From what the secretary said, Harmon is surrounded by a bunch of natural disasters. People from miles away are being evacuated and brought here," Ryan said. Just as he said that, two more ambulances showed up and quickly began unloading more injured people. "Come on, I have to check on my rookie," Ryan said, motioning for her to follow.

Abby followed slowly. She kept getting distracted by all the people there. Gathering thousands more people in Harmon while Alexander was free made her worry. Mostly she worried that this was his plan and that it was working brilliantly.

6

$\mathcal{R}$ yan went into a room at the end of the hall in the critical care unit. Abby hadn't been to Harmon General Hospital since the events that happened in the winter, and now she had been here twice in two days. Abby touched the wall as she walked by it, approaching the room. She recalled when her hounds painted the pure white walls red with the blood of Alexander's men. Although she hated her brother, she did admire his determination after being knocked down so hard just a few months before.

Gross, Abby thought as she shivered at the disgusting thought of admiring anything about Alexander. When Abby got to the door, she waited to be invited in out of respect. Ryan waved her over to the bed.

"This is Justin," he said, pointing to the young man on the bed with life support pumping away. He looked to be in his midtwenties. It was hard to tell because of how swelled and bruised his whole face was.

"What happened to him?" Abby asked. Ryan grabbed the young man's hand and looked disturbed by the state of him.

"No one knows. He was found just outside the station like this with his partner," Ryan replied in a pained voice.

"What room is his partner in?" Abby asked.

"The morgue," Ryan answered bluntly. Abby walked over to the other side of Justin's bed just as a nurse walked in. She greeted Ryan with a smile.

"How's he doing?" Ryan asked quickly.

"I'm so sorry, sir. Maybe I should grab you a doctor," she said softly.

"Just tell me," Ryan demanded. Abby was shocked at how rude Ryan was being to the nurse considering how polite he was before. The nurse took a deep breath before delivering the devastating news to Ryan.

"I'm so sorry, sir. His parents will be coming in later tonight to take him off life support. We did everything we could," she explained. Ryan turned away from her and looked at Justin. Both his eyes looked swollen shut, and there was dried blood around his mouth and ears. Abby watched the nurse slowly and awkwardly walked back out the room.

"I need to know what happened. Can't you tell like you did with the girl we found at the old Townsquare building?" he asked. Abby looked at Justin. His head trauma was so severe.

"I could, but it might kill him if he has a brain injury," she said.

Ryan put his hands on his head and yelled in frustration. His mind was so full of hate that it was overflowing. "He's already dead. He just won't be pronounced until his family takes him off the machine," Ryan said. He wasn't talking to Abby, but it seemed like he was trying to convince himself of this.

"Are you sure?" Abby asked before even touching Justin.

"Of course I'm not sure. I'm never sure about anything anymore!" he yelled.

Abby got closer to Justin and put her hands on each side of his head. As she dove into his recent memories, all the machines in the room began acting up and smoking, including the life support machine keeping him alive. Abby saw everything she didn't want to see. Her skin glowed, and her hair began to flame as she held on and watched the horrible events play out.

Ryan stood against the wall now and looked around as the lights in the hospital room flickered. Just as she let go of Justin's head, the faint sound of flatlining could be heard from the damaged heart monitor machine.

"You can tell me what happened in the car. We have to leave," Ryan said, grabbing Abby's arm and darting out the door. Abby's emotions were all over the place after becoming one with Justin and viewing his memories. With her mind so distracted, Ryan had to pull Abby out the hospital quicker. Nurses and doctors rushed toward Justin's room with crash carts while Ryan and Abby rushed the opposite way down the hall. Ryan knocked a few nurses over as he ran out of the hospital, still holding Abby by her arm.

Abby's adrenaline was pumping so hard. Just as they got to the lobby, two security guards locked the doors. Ryan slowed down when he saw them, but Abby kept going. She ran right through the glass doors without slowing down.

"Come on!" she screamed. Usually, it was Ryan always telling her to follow, but the tables have turned. Ryan ran through the broken door but got grabbed by one of the security guards. Without hesitation, he punched him directly on the face, causing him to drop. Instead of continuing to follow them, the second security guard tended to his partner on the ground.

Abby waited by the passenger door and got in as soon as he unlocked it. He threw the car into drive and got the hell out of there. They drove back to their old building.

"Well?" Ryan asked. "I certainly hope it was worth it," he said, hinting for Abby to explain what she saw.

"You're not going to like what happened," she said, hoping Ryan would choose the easy way out and ask her not to share.

"I need to know," he said firmly. Abby turned to Ryan and tried to figure out how to put what his young friend went through into words. "Justin got to the station right after the other officers had all been corrupted. When he questioned them all about where they were going, the chief ordered his officers to do it." She said all this slowly, trying to watch her words.

"To do what exactly?" he said with a look of terror on his face.

"Are you sure you want to know the specific details?" Abby asked, trying to spare him. He glared at her, waiting for her to tell him. "Fine. They beat him. Officers whom both of us have trusted beat them to death!" Abby shouted after being forced to say it. Ryan's face dropped. Abby could tell that he wanted to pull off the road for a moment, but he kept driving.

"I can't believe they would kill their own men," Ryan said, in shock.

"They were ready to shoot us with no questions asked too. But Alexander is in their heads. It's not actually them," Abby explained, trying to make Ryan feel better. He pulled into the driveway of their old apartment, but instead of getting out, he just sat there for a moment.

"Will they even remember?" he eventually asked. Abby looked at Ryan and reached over to unlock the doors.

"I really doubt it. The people at the courthouse didn't," she said as she exited the car. Abby put her bag on the trunk of the car and waited for Ryan to come out. He looked like he needed sleep and a lot of alcohol.

Ryan went to his door, expecting Abby to follow him, but instead, she went directly to Joe's door.

"What are you doing?" Ryan asked.

"I just need to ask him something," she replied. Joe opened the door quicker this time. He was showered; his golden hair was back in a ponytail again, but it was even brighter now that it was clean.

"Ms. Briggs," he said before he had even finished opening the door to see it was her.

"I have a favor to ask of you," she requested. Joe smiled and looked up at Ryan who was now standing inside his door across the hall, watching them.

"What can I do for you that this fine law enforcement officer can't do?" Joe asked sarcastically. Abby looked over at Ryan, who was looking angrier now.

"Can I keep Hecate here? She'll probably just sleep. I don't want to leave her alone across the hall when we go again," Abby asked.

"Of course," Joe said, taking the backpack off Abby's shoulders. "Where are you guys going?"

"None of your goddamn business," Ryan said firmly.

Abby ignored Ryan and replied, "We're not sure yet. I'll let you know." She leaned down and looked in the bag. Hecate was awake and silently looking up at her. Abby placed her lips on her forehead and gave her a kiss. Purring rumbled from the inside of the bag. "Thank you so much!" Abby said, running back over to Ryan's place.

Abby got inside and closed the door quietly behind her. It was completely dark, and she couldn't hear Ryan. "Uh, hello?" she said awkwardly but got no reply. She started feeling around on the wall for the light switch, but finally Ryan's voice was heard.

"No, leave it dark. My head is killing me," he said with a groan of pain.

"Why don't I let you get some sleep," she suggested. It was afternoon now, but in a few hours, it would be dark again. Ryan never said anything, but she heard heavy footsteps that led to his room and the sound from his bed when he dropped on it. Abby walked carefully through the living room to the balcony door and locked it. When she left, she grabbed his keys and locked the door. Before leaving, she paused for a moment with her left hand on the door. *Is leaving him here alone even safe?* she thought to herself. She looked across the hall at Joe's door. The knock must have startled him because he yelled "Shit!" right as it happened.

"Hey," he said, opening the door with a smile, probably hoping she hadn't heard him inside.

"I was wondering if you could do me another favor," said Abby.

"I'm not done doing your first favor yet, but sure, I'll watch him too," Joe said. Once he noticed what he had said, his face looked awkward. He laughed nervously.

"How did you know I was going to ask that?" she said.

"Damn good guess, eh?" Joe said jokingly.

"Can you call or text me on this number if you hear anything?" Abby said, handing him a small piece of paper before walking past him to the chair she sat on before, where the backpack was. She grabbed an old flip phone she used for emergencies out of it. To her surprise, Hecate was lying on the couch where Joe had clearly been sitting again. She looked completely relaxed around him, just like Abby was.

"Why don't you stay for a while. You'll be able to hear everything from over here anyway," Joe claimed. Although it was a good thought, she asked Joe to look after Ryan and Hecate because she wasn't sure if they were safe with her. She wasn't sure if anyone was safe with her anymore.

"No, I have to go," she said.

"To find Alexander?" Joe blurted out. There was a moment of silence as the words fell on their ears.

"How could you possibly know—" Abby started but was cut off.

"It's all over the news. Plus, you're in those rumors we were talking about too. It wasn't hard to put it together that you are that Abby," Joe said.

"How long have you known I was his sister?" asked Abby. Joe laughed and went to his fridge to grab a beer.

"I didn't. Until now, they were rumors like I said," he replied. Joe put the bottle between his teeth and bit the lid off before taking a huge gulp. "Wait a minute," he said as he walked into the bathroom, closing the door. Abby waited for him to come out and show her something important, but instead, she just heard the sound of him pissing hard-core.

All right then, she thought to herself, walking back over to Hecate on the couch. Abby looked behind her at the sword that Joe wouldn't let her see before. It almost looked like it was glowing now. It was the same sword and the same color of gold, yet somehow brighter. The lightning bolt at the base was now shimmering. Abby leaned over and touched it, but something crazy happened. As soon as her fingers made contact with the gold weapon, she was shocked. But not a normal shock; tiny streams of electricity attacked her hand, making her scream.

The sword glowed even harder now with a bright, blinding light. It looked like tiny lightning bolts were shooting out of it and into Abby. Abby got on her feet to try and pull away, but the electricity kept hold of her hand. Once she was able to get her hand away, it stopped. Abby ignored Joe yelling from the bathroom, asking if she was okay. Hecate had already run under the chair across the room.

Abby was furious and couldn't contain it. Her hair flamed, and her eyes glowed bloodred. She looked at the weapon, but unlike guns and regular sharp-edged weapons, the sword didn't melt. It wasn't a regular weapon. The bathroom door swung open just as everything went back to normal. Abby's hair had calmed down, but she closed her eyes, which were still glowing red, and turned around.

"What happened?" Joe asked. Abby rubbed her eyes and slowly opened them. They were back to normal now.

"Nothing, I thought I saw something," Abby said unconvincingly. Hecate was out now and purring around Abby's leg.

"I have to go," Abby said after lifting Hecate back onto the couch. She ran past Joe and slammed the door.

CHAPTER 7

*A*bby sat with the key in the ignition for a while before even starting the car. She had so many questions. Joe wasn't just some stoner like he was pretending to be. There was something more to him that he was keeping secret. Another reason why they were so similar: having deadly secrets. She wanted to go back and try with his head again, but he was so good at blocking it. Plus, it didn't seem like he was an evil-thought kind of guy other than the usual passing ones everyone had from time to time.

Abby started the car and left the building, hoping Ryan and Hecate would be safe. She kept her phone on full blast in case something happened and Joe tried to call. Abby decided to drive right to Townsquare. It was completely dark out, and colder night air had set in. Abby put all the windows down in the car as she drove to cool off. Every time her abilities set in, she always felt like she was overheating.

When she got to Townsquare, she parked the car on the edge of it. Abby took off her jacket and grabbed one of Ryan's hooded sweaters from the back seat. She put it on with the hood up so no one she had encountered before would try and stop her, and then she walked over to the new city hall building.

Abby peeked around the corner to the back of the building. All the abandoned police cars had been cleared out. Abby walked around the back. The pool where she fell when escaping in the winter was now gone, and it was just paved over for more parking on the grounds. Abby looked at the back door of the new city hall. The tape that read Caution, Keep Out had already been broken. *It could be kids,* Abby thought to herself. But she had to check anyway.

The door was unlocked and already a tiny bit open when she actually went to look. Abby looked around outside and at the far field of the building's grounds where the Harmon police had tried opening the sealed entrance to the tunnels. This whole area gave her a bad feeling again. Just a few days ago, her home was under her feet in this area, but now it felt different. *Alexander may not be here now, but he had been,* Abby thought to herself. She left quickly and closed the door tight.

Just as the cold night air hit her face again, so did something else. She turned around to see Chief Doyle standing beside her with his gun pointed at her. He ran it up her neck to her head. "It gives me no pleasure pulling this trigger, Abby," he said regretfully. Abby slowly turned her body to face him.

"Then don't do it," she said. The chief's mind had always been free from evil, but his thoughts now would make children cry. Abby went deeper and deeper into his head until he cringed and grabbed at it. Abby grabbed the gun while Chief Doyle was distracted by the pain.

Abby threw the gun as she ran back to the car, but when she got around to the front of the old Townsquare building, she was stopped and grabbed by a huge group of officers. Alexander must have freed them all from the tunnels. Abby didn't fight back; it was all she could do to keep her cool since the officers weren't themselves, but her hair ended up burning many of them.

Abby's skin kept getting hotter and hotter until none of the officers were able to even touch her. Abby wasn't paying attention to all the officers; one had grabbed a metal pipe. It melted a small amount on impact, but he was able to hit her violently over the head, knocking her unconscious.

Abby went in and out of consciousness as they dragged her back inside the Townsquare building. She could hear the officers mumbling but wasn't able to make out exactly what they were saying. As she woke up entirely, she noticed that her hands were both tied and there were chains around her feet. Abby pulled and pulled until the skin rubbed off her wrists. Her blood sizzled like acid as it ate through the rope with ease. Her wrists were freed, but the metal used for her feet wouldn't melt or budge. Abby started tugging at the chains on her ankles and ended up falling over. She looked up to see that the officers had all joined her in the large conference room.

"Alexander had prior commitments, but he sent one of his pets for you," said the chief as he walked through the crowd of officers and stood in front of them. Abby looked around. She was tied in the middle of the room with a view of all the doors, but nothing entered.

As she continued looking around, she heard something sliding across the floor. As it moved across the room toward her, she could sense the evil creature. It was a huge snake, but not a normal snake. When it came into view, Abby panicked. She'd never seen anything so ugly. It was about fifty feet long and had two heads growing out of its huge body. Abby wasn't sure what was worse, its obnoxious size or the number of heads.

The police watched as it got closer to her. Abby continued tugging at the chains binding her. "Those chains were brought here especially for you from your brother," the chief said.

Abby stopped pulling. It was clear she was stuck there until she could think of something. Her feet were useless now, but her hands were free. The giant snake was now beside Abby. As she looked back up from her feet, she saw its mouth open as it snapped at her. The fangs in its mouth were the size of her hands. She grabbed at one of its faces and burned it with her fuming temper, which was now radiating through her skin.

Its flesh melted, and small bits fell to the floor. Normally that would be enough to turn any threat away, but it only seemed to piss this particular creature off. It hissed and snapped again, just missing Abby's arm. She fell on her back, looking up at the snake, which was now on top of her. *Is this seriously how I'm going to die?* she thought to herself as the disgusting creature opened its mouth and lunged at her.

She closed her eyes, waiting for her fate, but it never came. Something fell through the ceiling and landed beside the snake. Debris fell on Abby and the police as most of the ceiling finished collapsing. Abby pushed most of it off her. The giant snake was already free from the rubble and was getting back up to finish the job. As it lunged at her again, its front half fell limp beside her. Heavy footsteps got closer and broke through the dust. It was Joe; he was in a golden armor and looked very different, his sword still wet with the green blood of the snake.

"Come on," he said.

"I can't get through these chains," Abby said, pointing to her feet. Joe swiftly copped through the chains with his sword; it cut through them like butter. The dust and debris had finally calmed down, and the police were finally able to see what had happened. They all drew their weapons and began firing. Joe pushed Abby behind him as his armor took all the bullets with ease. They kept firing until all Abby could hear were the clicks of empty guns.

Joe turned around and picked Abby up and flinging her over his back. He ran at lightning speed out the building and stopped at Ryan's car, which Abby had left at the edge of Townsquare. He placed Abby down, and she ran to the driver's side, unlocking all the doors for him to get in.

As Abby drove through the streets, she noticed it was much darker than usual. The streetlights were all out, and the only building lit up was the hospital in the distance, which was housing all the evacuated people from surrounding towns. Abby's head was so busy that she couldn't focus on anything. Joe remained quiet.

"Oh no," Abby said, remembering that Ryan was left alone.

"Hecate is with him," Joe said. Abby gave Joe a weird look and drove faster to the apartment building. She wasn't used to someone else reading her thoughts as quickly as she was having them. Abby pulled into the driveway and slammed the car into park. She ran into the building, worried about what she would find. At the other end of the hall by Ryan's, she saw some of the neighbors gathering.

"What's going on?" Joe asked, still sporting his armor. Abby was so concerned that she didn't even notice that Joe was right behind her. Some of the people in the hall looked at him like he was crazy because of what he was wearing, and they didn't answer him.

Finally, an older lady spoke up and said, "There's been gunshots and yelling and the sound of broken glass. The police don't answer right now," she answered in panic. Abby rushed in without thinking to find that most of Ryan's pictures had been smashed. There were large holes on the walls and cracks on the floor. It wasn't just yelling and glass breaking like the woman had said.

Joe entered slowly with his sword drawn. He looked around, shocked. Abby stepped over the cracks on the floor and went down the hall where Ryan's room was. She had no idea who could cause this much damage other than Alexander. Abby tried to walk into Ryan's bedroom, but the door was locked.

"Ryan?" she said quietly with a small knock on the door. Abby waited for a moment after she heard some movement in the room. The door unlocked. Joe finished looking around the apartment and walked down the small hall toward Abby. She slowly turned the door handle and reached around the corner for the light switch. When she switched it on, she found Ryan sitting on the bed beside Hecate, who was curled up on the bottom corner. His nose was bleeding, and his lip was swelling.

"What the hell happened?" Abby shouted, surprised at the sight.

"You might want to rephrase that question," Joe said quietly.

"Alexander happened," Ryan said, covering his eyes from the light that he didn't want. Abby looked around his room. Joe's eye followed hers. There were gunshots on the walls and broken glass everywhere. Abby concentrated on a small smudge of blood that looked like a hand mark.

"I think you got him," she answered.

"Not me," Ryan replied, looking down at the sleeping black cat.

"I'm pretty sure you need thumbs in order to use a gun," Abby said, thinking it was a joke. Ryan gave her a glare that made it clear her humor wasn't welcome at the moment.

"She grew until she looked more like a black panther with crazy fangs. She went for him and wouldn't stop until he fled," Ryan explained. "I never thought I would ever see that evil fuck actually run away from anything." Abby looked at Hecate who didn't look an inch bigger than when she left her. Ryan lay back down, still clutching his head, as Abby and Joe stepped outside the door for a moment to speak.

"We should probably drop him off at the hospital," Joe suggested. Abby looked back into the room. She wasn't sure if Joe just wanted to get rid of Ryan for a while or if he really thought medical attention was needed, but either way, she nodded in agreement.

Joe went back in to get Ryan, and Abby went into the living room. The bag that she had Hecate in was empty on the floor. Abby kicked away some of the broken glass from Ryan's family pictures. She grabbed all the contents of her bag she could find and then went back down the hall to Ryan's bedroom to get Hecate. Ryan was filling a small bag with a few items of clothing while Joe waited just inside the door.

"I'm surprised he agreed so easily," Abby whispered to Joe as she passed him in the doorway. Ryan finally grabbed his bag and walked to the door. He left to get in the car with the assistance of Joe. Abby scooped up Hecate and put her back in the bag. She left the apartment and locked up since Joe and Ryan were down the hall and almost outside. Abby ran to catch up. When they got to the car, she gently placed her bag in the back and went to the passenger side with Joe to help put Ryan in the car. Joe got in the back once they were done, and Abby quickly got in the driver's side and started the car.

She drove quickly out of the parking lot and through a red light at the intersection. Her thoughts were racing as they drove to the hospital. She wasn't sure if Ryan had gone completely bonkers or not. She looked back at her bag holding Hecate. In the few months she has had her, she had noticed some odd things, and it was clear she wasn't a normal cat. But growing into the size of a panther was something Abby thought she would have noticed once or twice. Ryan was slouched over in the back, holding his head. Abby wasn't even sure how to comfort him anymore.

Before long, they pulled into the hospital's lot. Abby drove around the lot twice only to find that there was nowhere to park. The hospital was even busier than it was before. Cars were parked on each side of the street. No one really worried about tickets since the police were missing.

Abby parked right at the front doors and helped Ryan into the hospital. Joe got in the driver's seat after helping Ryan out of the car and left to find a parking spot farther away. Abby walked to the reception with Ryan. Weeks before, Ryan had listed Abby as his emergency contact. Abby made sure to request that no visitors were allowed to see Ryan. The receptionist was friendly and agreed to the request. She marked on Ryan's file that if anyone were to come around asking for Ryan, Abby would get called immediately. A male in scrubs came behind them with a wheelchair and helped Ryan sit down.

"Head injury?" the guy asked.

"That's what he's here to find out," Abby said. The male smiled and walked away pushing Ryan, trying to communicate with him. Abby looked back to wave to Ryan, but he was hanging his head and couldn't see her. Abby turned around and looked back at the receptionist.

"I'm assuming it'll be a while with all the people that are here, eh?" she asked.

The receptionist typed something into her computer. "Yes, I'm afraid it will be hours until someone can even see him. We can give you a call when we have answers," she suggested politely.

"Okay, thank you," Abby said. The emergency room was just to the right of the main doors. Abby walked past it on the way out, and it was completely full. Abby got outside the hospital, relieved that Ryan was one responsibility off her shoulders at the moment. She looked back at the hospital. The glass they had busted earlier was already cleaned up. The guards who chased her and Ryan were off duty, and no one else seemed to remember her from earlier. With the number of people filtering in and out of the hospital, Abby really wasn't surprised.

She got over to the car and got in the passenger side. Joe look over at Abby and automatically started it.

"You haven't eaten anything in a while. Let's go back to my place and eat," he suggested. Abby looked at him for a moment, shocked that he would want to go back to the building where Alexander just attacked Ryan.

"Fine, but then you owe me a few explanations," Abby said firmly. Joe pulled out of the lot and got onto the main road.

"That's fair," he said with a smile. Abby looked out the window and didn't say anything about Joe speeding toward his building. Hecate was out of the bag now and was sitting on the back seat, looking at them. Her small fangs shined as the streetlights lit up her face. Abby grabbed Hecate under the front legs and lifted her onto her lap. She held her there as they drove.

Joe turned off the car and handed the keys back to Abby. Hecate held on while Abby carried her back into the building. Some neighbors were still in the hall talking but went quiet as the pair walked into the building. Abby paused at Ryan's door while Joe opened his. Abby placed her hand on Ryan's door. There was nothing wrong with it. Alexander seemed to have gotten in by breaking the glass door on the balcony.

Joe opened his door and waited for Abby to go in first. Abby went in and sat down on the foldout chair again and waited as Joe removed his armor and laid his sword across the coffee table in front of them. He went to the kitchen and asked Abby what she wanted.

"Answers," Abby replied. Joe came back out with a beer and opened it as he sat down. He grabbed his bong and lit it, taking a huge, long hit and blowing the cloud of smoke into the room they were in. The gold sword still shined and lit the room up more. Joe put his bong down and sat back, looking at Abby.

"So ask your questions," he said.

C H A P T E R

8

They sat in silence as Abby searched the thousands of questions in her mind for one to start with. "I guess we should start with basics. Who are you exactly?" she asked.

Joe sighed and sat at the edge of the couch. "Now there's a loaded question." He laughed.

"Then give me a loaded answer," Abby snapped. Her impatience was beginning to show.

"I'm pretty similar to you actually. My father is your father's brother," he replied. Abby wasn't even sure how to reply.

"Be more specific," she demanded.

Joe thought for a moment and then tried explaining to Abby. "There are many names for them throughout history. The most well-known would be God and the devil, or Zeus and Hades." Abby remembered all the books she and Ryan read about this in the library during the winter. That's where she found out that the hellhounds were naturally geared to being loyal to a female master.

"How long have you known?" Abby asked, trying to understand.

Joe smiled. "My whole life. The myths say that Zeus's wife, Hera, loves killing the offspring he creates outside of their marriage," he continued.

"Hera," Abby interrupted. That was a name she hadn't heard before.

"Hera, she's the goddess of marriage, family, fidelity—all the things that make her husband's bastard offspring the worst thing in the world to her." He continued, "My mother was in labor with me when she was struck and killed by lightning. Then on my sixteenth birthday, I was almost strangled in my bed by a man in a trance. He said Hera sent him. I fought him off, and since then, I've been doing everything I can to stay invisible."

Abby was in shock. Normally a story like this would sound absolutely crazy, but now it almost made sense. "The sword?" Abby pointed, not knowing how to add to this conversation.

"It was a gift from my father. It was made from a lightning bolt," he explained as he picked it up and smiled at it. "This is the first time I actually marched into battle with it," he said as he got up and grabbed a towel from the kitchen to wipe the blood of the giant snake off the blade.

"Thank you, by the way," Abby said. Joe smiled. "How did you know I was there?" Abby asked.

"Your blood," he replied.

"Pardon?" Abby said, confused.

Joe stood, leaned his sword against the wall where it was before, and sat back down. "It's the very reason why it's so hard to hide from people trying to find us. The smell of a god's blood is much different from mortals, especially for creatures sent to specifically hunt us. The smell of the weed in this place and the high clouding in my head has stopped them from finding me for a while," Joe explained. Abby took in what he was saying.

"And the armor? Where did that come from?" she asked. Joe looked at it on the floor.

"Same place, I guess. It just showed up here a few days ago, like someone knew I would be needing it," he said. Abby looked around, remembering that it used to be her old place.

"That's how Hecate showed up," she blurted out, "in this same apartment too." Abby jumped a bit, startled when Hecate jumped on her lap. Saying her name must have woken her up.

"I figured she was a gift too," Joe said. Abby kept looking down at Hecate and petted her. How could something evil be so cute? She looked back at Joe.

"Are you saying she was a gift from my father?" she asked with a worried look on her face. She loved Hecate now, but accepting a gift from the devil was definitely not her intentions.

"No, he's not really the gift-giving type. She's probably from Persephone," he continued. "Unlike Hera, Persephone doesn't wish death on Hades's other children outside their marriage, mostly because she's an unwilling party in that marriage and she feels horrible for anyone attached to Hades. She would be the master to the hellhounds in the underworld."

Abby looked away, trying to understand all this. Just when her life was going great, she gets thrown into another confusing mess. "Where did you learn all this?" she asked, impressed with his knowledge in this area.

"Everywhere," he said. "It's our lives. It doesn't matter if you learn about it through books, encounters, or near-death experiences. You just need to know what you're going to be up against."

"Why would Persephone give me Hecate?" Abby asked. "And why did your sword basically attack me when I tried to touch it?" Abby had so many questions, and she was spiraling. "And are there any more of those massive two-headed snakes around?" she asked, ending with the most important question.

"Wow, okay, here we go," Joe said, preparing his answers. "I don't know if any more snakes will come, but since it failed, probably not," he answered. "As for the sword, all gods are forbidden from stealing each other's powers. This is something that is also passed down to their children. And Hecate was probably given to you for protection. She's not just cute and cuddly."

Abby couldn't stop thinking of questions. "Wouldn't she have known that I had the hellhounds here already?" Abby asked.

"Yes, but she has thousands of hellhounds down there, and she's still a prisoner held in hell by Hades." Abby nodded, accepting that answer without knowing how to reply to it. There were so many more things going through her head, but Abby was finally hungry. Joe went into the kitchen and grabbed a bunch of things from his cupboards.

"Sorry, I don't have a lot here," he said, putting a few boxes of crackers on the table.

"Hold on," Abby said. She got up and placed Hecate on the couch beside Joe and left the apartment. Abby let herself into Ryan's place and went to his kitchen. She didn't want to spend time cooking, so she grabbed a container of cashews and a box of granola bars. On the way out, she snatched a bag of chips for Joe, thinking he may want the munchies with how much he's been smoking. She locked the door and went back into Joe's.

"Nice!" he said, smiling when she handed him the chips. Abby ate a granola bar and then went crazy on the cashews. Joe put the local news on to see what was happening in the area, and Abby went to call the hospital. She stood just outside the door. The neighbors who were chatting in the hallway had cleared now. A woman's voice answered. Once Abby confirmed her identity, she was told that Ryan was under morphine for pain control and that he would be staying there for a couple days at least.

Normally, being away from Ryan bothered Abby, but she was beginning to grow angered by his changing attitude. Abby came back into Joe's apartment and informed him of Ryan's condition. Joe even seemed relieved that Ryan would be away for a while.

"I really need to sleep, but I'm afraid that this isn't the best place to hide. I mean, I did use to live here," Abby said.

"I think it's a great place to hide. Why would you go to your old apartment, and how would you know the new occupant? It's better than you going across the hall. I doubt they would look for anyone here," Joe said, making a lot of sense.

"Would you mind then?" Abby asked. Joe shook his head and gave her the blanket that was hanging over the back of the couch he was sitting on.

"You can take the couch," he said, getting up and pulling a foldout chair. He grabbed a controller and started up a game, then grabbed his bong and put it beside his chair. The chips

Abby gave Joe didn't leave his sight and stayed on his lap. Abby fell onto the couch and started drifting off right away. She barely felt it when Hecate jumped back on the couch and cuddled into the blanket hugging Abby's feet.

Abby woke up and quickly saw the sun shining into the apartment. Unlike when she lived there, Joe didn't have blackout curtains up. She sat up and looked around. Joe wasn't there now, and the TV he was playing his games on was turned off. Abby got up slowly, trying not to disturb Hecate who was still in a heavy sleep. Abby grabbed a couple of things out of her bag. She walked to the bathroom and slowly opened the door. When she saw it wasn't occupied, she went in and cleaned herself up.

Just as she opened the bathroom door to come out, Joe burst in the door behind her, making her jump and yell. They both laughed.

"Didn't mean to scare you," he said. He was carrying a tray with two coffees on it and a couple of bags with pastries in them. "Breakfast?" he asked, holding up the items. Abby followed him over to the couch and sat on the other end of it while Hecate was slowly waking up on the middle cushion. Abby took a sip of her coffee and placed it on the coffee table.

"So—" Joe said.

"How long did I sleep?" Abby asked.

"About six hours," he replied.

"I'm so sorry. I only meant to lie down for an hour," she apologized.

"It's okay. I guess you needed it," he replied.

They both quickly finished their pastries. Abby rolled up the bag it came in, and Joe collected it to put it in the garbage with his.

"So we're cousins?" Abby asked, giving into another one of her questions from last night.

"Yes, we are. Our parents hate each other though. I'm surprised you're not more like your dad," he said.

"Isn't that a good thing considering who he is?" Abby said, giving Joe an odd look.

"Oh, of course! It's just odd. Usually, children born to the big three have their parents' personality embedded in them as the dominating trait," Joe explained.

"The big three?" Abby asked.

"Zeus, Hades, and Poseidon. It's rare for Hades and Poseidon to have mortal offspring. Zeus pollinated everywhere though. It's just rare for any of his kids to survive his wife's assassination attempts," he said.

Abby thought about it for a moment. It must have been difficult for Joe always having to be on the run and watching his back. "Why isn't Hades trying to kill me and Alexander?" Abby asked.

"Unfortunately, I don't know absolutely everything about them, but I doubt he really cares that you exist. I don't mean that in a harsh way either. It's just that neither of you are a threat to him," he explained. "If either one of you guys starts to gain more power than he's comfortable with, then I'm sure you'll be seeing him."

Abby turned and faced the blank TV, wondering if their father would ever put a stop to Alexander. Joe noticed Abby looking at the TV and put it on, changing the channel to the local news. Even though both Abby and Joe had seen that the police had gotten out of the tunnels, the local news station was still reporting that the officers continued to be missing.

"They're probably still hiding in that stupid building," Joe yelled at the TV. He was probably right; the old Townsquare building seemed to be a hot spot for Alexander's evil plans.

"I wonder what they're waiting for though," Abby said, thinking about the news story in front of them.

"I'd have to say that they're waiting for Alexander's orders," he replied. His hatred for the police was something that was very obvious in his tone whenever he referred to them.

Abby and Joe sat in silence for a while, both thinking about what to do next. It seemed like Joe was already making it his responsibility to help his newly found cousin. As they were weighing out their options, they heard a huge smash out the front of their building on the main road. Abby and Joe ran out of the building, slamming the door behind them. People from their building and other pedestrians were already gathering on the sidewalk.

There was smoke everywhere. Two cars had gotten into a huge accident right outside. A man climbed out of a smoke-filled car while a woman remained trapped in a totaled minivan. She yelled for help, but no one went near the car once it began flaming out of the front end. It only took seconds for the whole car to become engulfed in flames.

Abby ran to the car. People yelled at her from the side of the road to stay back. Abby opened the driver's side door, and as she did, it fell off its hinges, and she threw it out of the way. Abby looked at the trapped woman, who was now losing consciousness because of the amount of smoke surrounding her.

The woman's bottom half was crushed under the mangled portion of her car. Abby bent down and kept pushing as hard as she could to free the woman. Abby moved it a few inches, just enough to free her. Right as Abby got her out of the car, the flames grew larger into an explosion. Abby bent down, shielding the woman from the blast. Both cars were now completely on fire, and smoke filled the street. Abby looked around; the smoke was so thick that she couldn't even see across the street.

Abby picked up the woman, and she held her high as she walked through the flames. Fire was an old friend of Abby's and would never hurt her. She finally got within view of all the citizens on the sidewalk. Abby gently placed the woman on the sidewalk and looked around for Joe. He was standing with the other guy, who was able to get out of his car.

"Did I just watch her walk through fire?" the man asked Joe as Abby got closer. Joe smiled and looked at Abby.

"How is she?" Joe asked.

"Unconscious," Abby responded. The sirens of the ambulance could finally be heard coming. With the number of people at the Harmon General Hospital, it was surprising that they had any ambulances available at all.

"Maybe before they get here to check you two out, you should repeat what happened once more," Joe said as he looked at Abby and pointed at the man, gesturing for her to listen to his story.

"We both came from Townsquare. I work in a small shop just outside of it. I'm not sure about the lady. I tried cutting through Townsquare to get there early today, and all of a sudden, actual police officers were shooting at my car," he said emotionally.

"Harmon police officers?" Abby asked.

"I don't know, but they were in uniform. They looked crazy. The look in their eyes wasn't normal. And it wasn't just me! They shot at everyone in sight. Then it seemed like something dark was chasing us as we drove off. We went as fast as we could. I think that's why me and the lady in the minivan weren't paying attention to each other," he said, now crying. Joe was much nicer to people than Abby ever was.

"You two were too busy running for your lives. It sounds terrifying," Joe said as he embraced the emotional man. The ambulance skidded up to the side of the road. They tended to the woman first, then ran to help the man with Joe. A female paramedic stopped to ask Abby if she was okay.

"Yes, I wasn't involved," Abby said.

"Members of the crowd said you were in the flames and would need help with burns," the paramedic said as she looked at Abby's arms, which didn't have a single mark on them.

"It all happened so quick. People get confused," Abby said. The female paramedic walked away and spoke with her male coworker, and they looked back at Abby. Before they could ask any more questions, Abby went back inside the building and into Joe's apartment. Hecate was right by the door, waiting.

"The police are going nuts, Hecate," Abby said as she reached down to pet her adorable friend. Abby sat inside and turned on the news again. There was still no mention of the police being out or the accident that just happened.

"How reliable," Abby said, shutting the TV off and throwing down the remote on the coffee table. Abby wasn't sure what the darkness could be or why it would be chasing random people out of Townsquare. Alexander was always full of tricks, but none of what was happening even made sense. The storms and natural disasters all around them causing surrounding towns to be evacuated into Harmon seemed a little too convenient.

Even though all this stuff was terrible, Abby had to wonder about a few things. If Alexander could pull these kinds of things off, could Abby actually affect her surroundings the way Alexander does? Could she match his power, or a better question, would she even want to? And if she could affect her surroundings, was this why Ryan was changing? They had been spending most of their time together over the last few months. Abby wasn't sure what to believe anymore.

Voices filled the hallway, making it obvious that the crowd from outside was beginning to dissipate. Abby listened as everyone walked in, still talking about what had happened. Joe came in and went straight for his bong. Hecate jumped on the coffee table across the two of them and sat there looking at both their faces.

While Joe got high to relax after those events, Abby went over to Ryan's to grab some cat treats she had forgotten over there. When she came back, Hecate was freaking out and yelling for them. She gave her a handful and sat back down. Everyone was beginning to relax now.

"We have to go to Townsquare, don't we?" Joe asked in an exhausted voice.

"Unfortunately," Abby replied.

They both sighed and sat there for a while, thinking about what lay ahead for them.

C H A P T E R

9

The door slammed. Joe was running back and forth to the car, loading his armor and weapons into it. It turned out he didn't have a shortage in blades. His closet went completely unnoticed the whole time Abby and Ryan were in Joe's place, and now she knew why. The knives and sword he had hidden in there were unlimited, it seemed.

"I'm just bringing the best ones," he said as he came in for another load.

"Are you bringing that one?" Abby asked, pointing to the golden lightning sword that saved her from the giant snake.

"Always, but that stays at my side," he said as he walked over and picked it up, then set it by the door.

Abby grabbed another set of clothes from her bag. Her jacket was still on the chair where she left it. She went into the bathroom and looked at herself. She hadn't even brushed her hair today yet. Lucky for her, her cousin had long hair too. She grabbed a brush from a shelf over the toilet and brushed her long red hair out. She put on a new pair of jeans and another black tank top and came out. Hecate was sitting on the couch, watching them get ready. Joe came back in.

"Everything is packed in the car," he said.

"You're not planning on using those weapons on the cops are you?" she asked, shocked that he was supposed to be the better half of this duo.

"Only if we have to. Gotta be prepared," he said.

Joe kicked off his shoes and walked out of his pants. He reached into a drawer and pulled out a few pieces of clothing. "I just need to take a quick shower," he said. He took his hooded sweatshirt off. Because of how baggy his clothing always was, Abby never noticed just how built Joe was. His biceps were the size of her head.

He shook his hair out, and it shined with a golden ray. He went into the bathroom and closed the door. It wasn't hard for Abby to believe they were related; he was just the complete opposite of her and Alexander, which was perfect.

Abby sat down, petting Hecate on the couch while the water for the shower ran. She had grabbed her coat and was ready to go. Abby leaned over and grabbed her bag. She opened it on the couch beside Hecate, and she freely jumped in and began purring. Abby had already put her blanket in so she would be comfortable.

A knock on Ryan's door across the hall jolted Abby and Hecate. Abby walked over to the door and looked through the peephole. It was just the building's superintendent and the maintenance man. Abby went out and greeted them.

"We're here to make some of the repairs," the maintenance man, who was wearing blue, said.

"Ryan's still in the hospital. I didn't think he would be able to call anyone," Abby replied as she put the key in the hole.

"The neighbors called after the break-in happened. It's crazy what's going on out there again, eh? I'm moving my family again from here," the superintendent said, engaging Abby in conversation. Abby had never been a fan of the useless superintendent of that building. His whole demeanor made it obvious he didn't care about anything but himself.

Abby slowly backed away from them toward Joe's door until she was able to say "Have a nice day!" while closing the door. She got back into the living room to find a uniformed police officer staring at her through the open window. She recognized him as one of the officers Ryan worked shifts with often, but she couldn't remember his name. There were too many officers to remember.

Before Abby thought of anything else, she grabbed the bag holding Hecate and put her outside the front door where it was safe. The worker and the superintendent were already inside Ryan's place. Abby walked back into the living room to find that the cop wasn't there anymore. She peeked her head through the window and was grabbed by the neck.

Abby's skin flared, but the officer was still able to pull her out the window and throw her on the ground even as his hand burned. Abby looked up at the officer, who was now pointing a gun right at her head. Abby stared straight down the barrel. Abby grabbed the gun; her steaming-hot skin melted it enough for her to bend it. But it seemed like Joe wasn't the only one with the idea to bring more than one weapon.

The officer grabbed at his thigh and pulled another gun out. Trees shielded the altercation from public view. Abby looked at the gun, but before she had time to do anything, Joe grabbed the gun and snapped it in half with ease. His hair was finally clean, and it was so much more golden and brighter than ever before. He only had half a god's blood in his veins, but he looked like a pure, real god. He picked up the officer by the neck and threw him so far away that Abby didn't even hear him hit the ground nearby.

"Are you mad I killed him?" Joe asked while holding his hand out to help Abby up. Abby wanted to be mad, but she was almost ready to kill him herself.

"I'll get over it," she said, accepting his hand and rising to her feet. As Abby got closer to the open window she was pulled out of, Hecate jumped on the ledge and meowed at her.

"I guess you found her, eh?" Abby said, surprised at how connected the three of them seemed to be. Joe nodded. Abby went to climb through the window again, but Joe took her by the arm.

"Why don't we just take the doors this time?" he said, laughing. Abby smiled and walked inside with him awkwardly.

The first thing Joe did when he got back inside was to close and lock the window in his apartment.

"Do you think it's a coincidence that we both lived in this apartment?" Abby asked. Joe laughed while he placed a drumstick in the window to secure it more.

"There are no such thing as coincidences," he replied. Abby shook her head at herself. *Of course there isn't,* she thought. Abby was still a little in shock about being attacked by the officer, and she wondered if Ryan would be safe around Joe now. It seemed like he was more than ready to kill a cop. Joe was ready to go, but before leaving, he sat down near his regular end of the couch and smoked his bong again. He coughed for a few minutes, then walked to the door and looked back at Abby, who was just sitting in a foldaway chair staring off into the distance, lost in thought.

Joe's fingers snapped, startling Abby from her daze. Abby quickly grabbed her coat and met Joe at the door.

"Are you okay?" Joe asked, looking at Abby's wondering eyes.

"Yeah, I guess I'm just bummed out that this is happening," Abby admitted.

"Hopefully we can all move on with our lives after we find Alexander again," Joe said, trying to comfort his cousin.

Abby grabbed Hecate and held her in her arms instead of placing her back in the bag. They walked to the car, which was parked in the back lot.

"So this is your boyfriend's car, right?" Joe asked as he got in the passenger side. Abby got in the driver's side and reached around to put Hecate in the back.

"Yeah," she answered blandly.

"Are you two serious? Is there a wedding?" Joe asked.

Abby turned on the car and paused, unsure of how to answer. "No, it's not the same anymore," Abby said.

"Do you want to talk about it?" Joe asked. Abby shook her head as she began to drive.

"The accident has been cleaned up," Joe said, changing the awkward subject. Abby looked over. All the broken car pieces had been cleaned up quickly. Abby drove on, but the closer she got to Townsquare, the more problems they saw. There were many cars that had crashed into one another, but the emergency response workers who were left weren't going near the center of town. Instead, people were racing away from Townsquare.

A car raced toward Abby and Joe head-on, smoke pouring out from under its hood. Abby swerved enough to miss it, and it crashed into a telephone pole behind them.

"Should we stop and help?" Joe asked, but Abby just kept driving. Abby drove around Townsquare and kept going.

"What's happening?" Joe asked.

"If the police station is still empty, then we can grab some of the chief's special stock," Abby said. Joe rolled his eyes. He didn't like cops and definitely didn't want to go to the station.

Abby pulled into the driveway, skidding around the corner and parking swiftly. She got out of the car without words and without waiting for Joe. Joe ran to catch up with her. The door was locked, which was expected.

"Oh well, I'm sure we have enough anyway," Joe said, encouraging Abby to turn around and go back to the car with him. Abby touched the door handle and focused all her hatred on the tiny object. Within seconds, the solid brass door handle became nothing but a melted soggy mess dripping down the door. Abby kicked the door open after melting the lock. Joe watched in amazement.

The police station was completely empty. Abby walked to the chief's office. The door was unlocked. She opened it and walked around to his desk. She looked through the drawers. Joe came to the door and watched. Before he could ask what she was looking for, she straightened up and closed the drawer, holding a bunch of keys she found. Abby walked past Joe in the doorway and stopped at a small door directly beside the chief's office. She tried a bunch of the keys until she found the right one.

"Why not just melt it like you did before?" Joe asked.

"Because there is a key," Abby snapped. She wasn't trying to show off; she only used her abilities when they were truly needed. Abby walked in and left the door open for Joe. The room was filled with different things.

"Here," Abby said. Abby walked over to the right corner of the room and pulled the covers off a small shelf. On the shelf were enough explosives to blow up half the city of Harmon. Abby took a few items from the shelf and left. Joe looked around.

"I prefer my blades," he said as he walked out the room, turning his nose up at the explosives.

"You can't deny that they might come in handy," Abby said. Her only goal was to finally kill Alexander. She didn't care how she did it. She just wanted to correct her mistake from the winter—she never should have let him live.

Abby locked the door to the ammunition room again and tossed the keys on Chief Doyle's desk. She walked out of the station with Joe beside her. Just as they got to the car, Joe noticed that a few cars were pulling over to the police station's parking lot.

"Look," Joe said, pointing at the cars. They were police cars from the surrounding cities that were evacuated into Harmon. Abby started the car and drove out of the lot, trying not to look suspicious. The last thing she and Joe needed was a shoot-out with some substitute cops.

As they drove out of the police station, Abby looked down the road leading out the city. It was true; in the distance, there was complete blackness because of all the natural disasters surrounding Harmon. There were visible funnel clouds in the distance hovering over one of the neighboring towns. Abby was shocked to see some members of the public outside their homes in that area. They were taking pictures of the mysterious weather on their phones. People never seem to know what's going on around them unless they see it through the screen of their phones. The human race was a mystery to both of them. Joe looked at Abby and rolled his eyes at the people.

Abby got back on the road and headed toward Townsquare. The gunshots in the distance almost sounded like fireworks. They drove toward the danger. Just as they turned down the main street that connected with Townsquare, a uniformed police officer jumped at their car. He barely acted human anymore and had no concern for his own safety.

The officer landed partly on the hood of the car and the windshield. Abby slowed the car down. He was another officer whom she recognized. He looked into the window at Abby and Joe and began punching the window. His knuckles tore open as he cracked the glass. Abby tried speeding up and shaking him off the car, but nothing worked. He began digging into the splintered glass. Blood smudges were everywhere as he clawed his way into the car. Joe grabbed his sword, ready for a battle if he got in. The officer's face looked deranged.

"Hold on," Abby said. She sped the car up super fast and then slammed on the brakes. The officer was thrown from the windshield and across the road. Abby waited for a few seconds, but he never got up.

"I guess we both got one," Joe tried to joke. You'd think that being connected to more evil would mean that Abby was the colder one who didn't value human life, but Joe had been hurt way too much after growing up in the foster system. Abby knew all about that, but hurting her was a bit more difficult. Joe's abilities didn't run almost entirely on emotions. He could think while he was in battle. Abby had to rely on her instincts. The more angry and full of blinding hatred she was, the more powerful she became. It proved to be annoying in the past, but Abby was hoping that this time, her hatred for Alexander would be the thing fueling her abilities.

Joe and Abby were so busy staring at the body and waiting to see if he would get back up that they didn't even notice that the car had stalled. After loading the car with everything they needed, they forgot to check one thing: if they had enough gas. They had passed quite a few gas stations on the way, but none of them were open even though it was early afternoon now. Abby looked through the trunk. Ryan was always prepared for all types of situations. She moved Joe's armor to the side, and there was a small container of gas Ryan had put there for emergencies. Abby took it out and partly closed the trunk. She opened the gas cap and poured it in. When she was done, she threw the container back into the trunk and slammed the trunk close.

"Give me your keys," Abby heard as she felt a blade on her neck. She turned around slowly to see two men with ski masks on standing there. Abby had gotten completely tired of these thugs acting like they owned Harmon whenever something went wrong. Joe quickly got out of the car, but Abby put her hand up at him to wait.

Abby closed the hand holding the keys, then opened it, and quickly handed the keys to one of the men. He was so focused on the car that he didn't noticed steam coming from the keys. As soon as Abby dropped them on his hand, he screamed and let the keys go. The other man tried grabbing them from the ground in front of Abby, but she kicked him in the head as he kneeled down. Both the thugs ran off while helping each other and holding each other up.

"That was quick," Joe said, laughing. Abby picked the keys up and got back in the car. She didn't fully melt them, so they kept their form. She put the key in the ignition after it cooled down and started the car.

"I actually feel a lot better," Abby admitted. Joe laughed and put his hand on her shoulder playfully.

"You can't hold all that in," he said. Abby felt completely relaxed and ready to face new challenges.

CHAPTER

10

*T*he car crept along the curb. Abby stopped and put it into park. She could barely see through the screwed-up windshield while she was driving there. They parked just down the road from Townsquare so they wouldn't be noticed. The new city hall building was in distant view. Abby grabbed Hecate from the back seat and put her in the bag again. She zipped it all the way this time. Joe went around to the trunk of the car with his glowing sword in his hand and began putting on his armor. Abby waited while Joe got together the weapons he was bringing. He lightly closed the trunk, trying not to cause much noise that would draw any attention to them.

They walked down the street surrounded by nothing but darkness. It wasn't even nighttime. The storms surrounding Harmon were slowly getting closer. Abby looked up. The storms weren't even following wind directions; they were just all being pulled toward Harmon. Darkness was slowly closing in on the city. No one should have ever been evacuated to Harmon. Waiting out the storms in their own homes would have been safer than coming to this city.

Distant gunshots continued to get louder as they approached Townsquare. Abby walked down an alley parallel to Townsquare.

"Where are you going?" Joe asked quietly. Abby put her index finger to her mouth, signaling him to be silent. She walked into a dark, narrow alley between two small stores that were currently closed, much like the rest of the businesses in and around Townsquare. At the end of the alley, there was a fence separating them from Townsquare. Abby looked through the slats of the fence to try and see what they were going to be dealing with.

Abby looked back at Joe, who had joined her at the fence. As much as he tried to be quiet, his armor didn't cooperate. The look of shock on Abby's face as she looked back through the fence made Joe quickly look through the fence as well. The two looked on at a battleground. There were bodies lying on the ground— innocent citizens that were gunned down by their own city's police force—as deranged police officers walked and marched around them. There were so many cops outside—fifty, maybe sixty. Most of the officers were coming out of and surrounding the new city hall building.

After Joe was able to pull his eyes off the innocent casualties, he asked, "Should we just fight our way in?" His voice was blunt, like the sight upset him more than he was letting on to Abby. Evil thoughts ran through Joe's head and made Abby aware of his intentions. He didn't only want to kill Alexander but the officers too. It didn't seem to matter to him that they were under Alexander's influence; he just wanted to kill them for their actions.

"As much as I'm losing my cool with them, I want to try to keep as many of the cops alive as possible," Abby said, trying to shut down Joe's thoughts.

"Other than the two we already took care of, right?" Joe said with a snicker. Abby didn't reply but gave him an angry look.

"Save the anger for your brother," he said. Abby looked back through the fence at all the dead bodies lying around.

"That's exactly what I'm doing. He's the one we want, not the officers that he's just using," Abby explained.

"I understand that, but if it's them or us, I'm not waiting for them to strike first just because you want to do the right thing," Joe said firmly. He was probably right. This wasn't the time for morals; this was turning into a war.

Abby and Joe walked around to the entrance of Townsquare. Cars were smashed up all over the place with the occupants lying dead inside them. The cars were covered in bullet holes. Some of them were still fresh, steam still coming out from under their hoods.

"Okay, so how do we get past these police zombies and get to Alexander?" Joe asked, looking around at the loss of life that Alexander once again caused.

"This is all my fault," Abby said as she looked around emotionally.

"No, it's not," Joe said, trying to make her feel better.

"It is! I could have killed him before and should have," she said. As much as she appreciated her cousin trying to calm her down, it wasn't helping. He was speaking about things he had no idea about; he wasn't there in the winter.

Abby counted seven people lying dead on the street with another three dead in their smashed-up vehicles.

"I can't believe this is happening," Abby said. She was wishing Ryan was there—not the new aggressive Ryan, but the one whom she fell for, the one she could actually talk to.

"It's time to make things right then," Joe suggested to Abby. Abby tried clearing her mind and coming up with a plan of attack.

"We have to get into that building," Abby said, nodding her head at the new city hall building—the building she hated most in the whole city.

"There's no way we would get into the new city hall building without having to kill a bunch of the officers," Joe said.

"I know. There are too many of them," Abby said. "Although ..."

Joe looked at her, intrigued.

"Since Alexander is likely in there, if they were to capture us, there's a good chance that's were they would take us," Abby said.

Joe looked torn about the idea. "That could work, I guess," he said, unconvinced. "Unless they execute us first," he continued, finally sharing his doubt. Abby walked out, about to walk directly into the sight of the marching officers.

"It's a risk I have to take. I owe it to all these people," she said, looking back at Joe and pointing to the bodies on the ground and in the vehicles.

Abby kept her head up even as officers from the other side of Townsquare starting yelling and charging at her. She just walked toward them, waiting for her capture. Joe waited a moment, still unsure of the plan. He put his sword in the holder on the side of his armor and walked with Abby. The police closed in on them. As they got closer, Abby could see the details of their faces. Their eyes were red and bloodshot; darkness surrounded their eyes as well. Their lips were cracked too. *I guess Alexander doesn't even let them have water breaks,* Abby thought.

The officers screamed for Abby and Joe to get on their knees. Abby complied, hoping it would lead her to Alexander. Joe was less than enthusiastic about falling to his knees as ordered and was hit on the back of the knees with a baton before kneeling with Abby.

"We could have just fought our way in," Joe said roughly as he fell to his knees. Joe was clearly hating this plan so far. The officers waited for a moment, almost like they were waiting for orders. Within moments, officers grabbed Abby by the arms and walked her roughly inside. There were multiple officers holding her on each side of her body, and it was taking every bit of self-control she had not to start burning their faces off. Abby looked back to see that Joe was walking with his head down; his fists were clenched. It was clear that he was waiting for the moment he could attack.

They walked around to the back of the building. Abby looked up; there were many more faces staring at her from the windows of the new city hall building. She looked up at the top window— the window she had to jump out of back in the winter in order to get to safety. Alexander had always seemed to be drawn to this building. *What's so special about this building?* she thought to herself, wondering why it was so significant.

One of the officers went first and opened the door. Abby was roughly pushed inside the building. She looked around.

"So where is he?" she asked the officers bluntly. They pointed up the stairs without speaking to her. Just then Joe was shoved through the door as well, joining his cousin again.

"I'm finding it harder and harder to believe you're against killing these assholes," Joe said with his hand on his sword. A cop Abby didn't recognize noticed Joe's hand on the sword and ordered him to put his hands up and surrender his weapon. Joe had a goofy smile on his face as he put his hands behind his head and said "Try it" to the cop. The cop walked beside him as other officers watched and grabbed the handle of Joe's sword. The officer screamed in pain as the sword lit up with electricity at his touch just as it did with Abby. The officer couldn't let go willingly and was thrown back by the strong currents running through his body. He fell onto the ground and didn't get up.

Abby looked as a couple of officers went to his side. His head was almost entirely blackened, and the burns stretched up his arm. He was dead and cooked to a medium rare. Abby looked at Joe, who was now looking extremely proud of himself.

"They're under Alexander's trance. I told you we can't steal one another's abilities," he said, referring to his earlier explanation. They were only human, but they had Alexander in their head. It was odd to see what touching his sword did to a mortal body when it didn't leave a mark on Abby. It was a strong warning for her, but not a deadly one.

"That's three now," Abby said, referring to the number of cops they've already been forced to kill.

"You're going to have to stop counting," Joe said.

Abby and Joe walked up the stairs to the second level. The cops who escorted them inside slowly followed them while a few others kept looking at the officer's body.

"What floor?" Ryan asked loudly, yelling back at the officers behind them. The officers didn't reply to him with words but merely pointed at the stairs again.

"He's on the top floor or roof, I think," Abby said.

"You can sense him? I can't yet," Joe replied.

"We're much more connected," Abby said. She and Alexander were definitely connected in many ways. Abby looked around as they slowly climbed the stairs. The building no longer smelled like fresh paint; now it smelled like ashes. There were bloodstains on the walls as they passed. Abby touched them. She could feel the fear that one of the officers had as he accidentally woke up from Alexander's trance, not knowing where he was or what he was doing, then lying on the ground against the wall, wondering why his own fellow officers shot him and left him to bleed to death.

Abby quickly took her hand away from the wall. *This building shouldn't even be standing anymore,* she thought. There was way too much evil that was held within its walls; it needed to be burned to the ground.

Abby got to the top floor first. It was completely dark. She walked forward and found the metal stairs leading to the roof and climbed them. It was so dark that she wasn't even sure if Joe was following her. Abby touched the straps of her backpack. It made her feel better knowing Hecate was with her and not left alone somewhere. Abby got to the top, but she was blocked by a steel door that was stuck. She used her shoulder and forced it open.

There was a bit of natural light now but not much because of the amount of darkness surrounding them. It continued getting closer and closer. Abby looked around. She sensed that Alexander was there, but she couldn't see him. She heard noises behind her and looked back at the door. Joe was joining her on the roof. He slammed the door behind him as hard as he could. The officers who were following them pounded on the door, trying to open it, but it was stuck even harder now.

"Now we're probably stuck too," Abby said sarcastically. Joe laughed with an uneasy edge. It was clear he was very uncomfortable there.

"I'm sure I can break it, or you can melt it," he said, looking back at the door. Abby walked around the roof. It was large, and there were a few ledges and different levels that would make it easier for Alexander to hide—not that he would need help now that he can just suck himself under their feet.

The new city hall building was one of the tallest buildings in Harmon. Abby stopped for a moment and looked over the ledge at the city. She could almost see it all. Any other time during the last few months, it would have been beautiful; but now that Alexander was free again, it wasn't a nice sight at all. The violence and destruction were stemming from Townsquare now. Cars farther away were set on fire. Actually, there were smoke coming up from multiple small fires. Bodies were scattered on the streets. The emergency workers who were left didn't seem like they were willing to risk coming to this part of town now. It wouldn't be surprising if they all went home to their families after all they had seen that day.

Before, Alexander wanted to create an underworld where he could rule using the tunnels in the city. Now it seemed like he wanted to create hell on earth. Joe came back and joined Abby, looking out at Harmon being destroyed once again. Joe patted Abby on the back as he approached. His hand gently touched the backpack. A small purr came out of her bag. Abby didn't open it; she was still unsure of her surroundings.

"Why isn't he here?" Abby asked. It was a rhetorical question, but Joe replied anyway.

"Why else would he get his minions to bring us here? He was probably here before," he said. Abby looked around at the grounds again. The bodies were still there, but the officers were no longer walking around. All the officers were inside now. The only officers she saw were the ones coming back from hanging around Ryan's car, which she left around the corner.

"Something is wrong," Abby said. Her head was filled with horribly evil thoughts, and she could sense a huge amount of evil coming their way. Joe looked over the side and then grabbed Abby by the arm.

"We have to go," he said as he pulled her roughly.

"What the hell?" Abby yelled.

"Smell the air. Smell it!" Joe shouted. Abby looked around and smelled the air around her. It was faint, but the smell of gasoline was obvious.

"I saw them pushing in barrels," he said. "This was just a trap." They ran down the stairs; his grip was still on her arm. Abby pulled her arm out of his grasp.

"I think I get it now," she said, following him willingly. Their steps got louder the faster they ran. Joe threw his whole body into the door, and it busted open. The cops who were still standing on the other side of the door fell down the stairs with the door. Abby followed Joe down the stairs. They both fought the urge to stop and take time to check on the obviously dead officers.

The bottom floor was completely filled with Alexander's cops. They turned around and looked at them slowly, completely in sync with one another. Abby stopped a few steps up and looked at the crowd staring at them. Each one of them had a piece of Alexander in their head; there was so much evil in one room. She wasn't sure why they weren't swarming them already. Joe slowly motioned for Abby to come down. She did, but she stopped and pointed at what she saw. The barrel that Joe saw the cops pulling in was added to the many barrels that were already inside. One of the officers was struggling to use his fatigued coordination to flick a lighter.

"But you'll all die!" Abby screamed at the crowd.

"Come on," Joe said, this time just nudging Abby instead of grabbing her arm. Joe ran down a hall leading away from the large room and the back door. Abby ran behind him, holding on to the straps of her bag, trying to keep Hecate secure. They got to the front door, but Chief Doyle was standing in front of it. The kind, gentle man who never had terrible thoughts was now full of Alexander's evil, and it didn't match him. His face was much more pained, and his eyes were the darkest out of every other cop they had seen there.

"Chief, please, try and think," Abby pleaded. Within a second of Abby speaking to him, the chief pulled out a gun and shot Joe. The pressure from the short-range shot knocked Joe over. Abby fell to his side. Before even checking to see if Joe was injured, her heart raced and her skin burned. Joe looked at Abby as she burned into her full power. Apparently, family really brought out the fire in her.

Before Chief Doyle could even think about getting another shot at one of them, Abby's eyes glowed, and she raised her hand in a tossing motion at the chief. A speeding fireball hit the chief, sending him flying backward. He busted through the door and landed somewhere outside.

"I'm fine," Joe said, trying to calm Abby down. Abby flung off her bag and gave it to Joe. Her eyes were still glowing, her skin shined, and her hair flamed. There was no calming her down now, but before they could even get to the door, a small explosion rumbled through the whole building.

"Here I thought that my only chance of dying in fire would be if we had a disagreement," Joe tried to joke while facing his death. Abby couldn't stop thinking about her anger; it kept her fire ignited. The main explosion filled the whole main floor with fire. Abby leaned over Joe and Hecate; the explosion didn't even move her. Flaming debris fell around them. The stuff that hit Abby just burned into ash on touch. Abby dragged Joe out of the burning building while he held Hecate in the bag. They got outside just as the whole building collapsed. Dust and smoke rose from the pile of debris as the collapsed building hit the ground.

Joe got up and checked his armor for any damage. The gunshot didn't even leave a dent. Abby closed her eyes and calmed herself down. Once her mind was clear of the hate fueling her fire, she was able to look around and see other things, like the loss of life that just happened. Alexander just blew up most of the remaining officers in Harmon—innocent people who were just under his trance. Abby walked up close to the flames, closer than anyone else could go. She touched the flames and looked at her skin. It was still pale white.

"Abby?" Joe said. He was still standing back from the fire.

"It's not fair. They didn't have to die," she said, still running her hand through the flames.

"Stop doing that," Joe said. Abby smirked.

"Fire can't kill you when you were born in flames," Abby said. Joe stepped back and bumped into people. A small crowd had formed behind him. A fire truck came speeding into Townsquare.

"I guess people were only scared of this building and the cops," Joe said just loud enough for Abby to hear him. The fire truck only had two firefighters inside; it was likely hard to get that many who would be willing to volunteer to go near Townsquare.

Abby turned to walk away from the fire. As she turned around, the crowd of people screamed. Abby grabbed her long red hair and pulled it around to look at it. It wasn't flaming anymore, and she was calm. She looked up at Joe, who looked like he was pointing through her. She turned around. Behind her, inside the raging fire, was a male silhouette walking toward them. He stopped once he got to the edge of the flames but stayed within it. People were backing up and screaming but most continued to look. Humans are a curious race.

The details of his face got into focus more now that he was closer. It was Alexander. His laugh made Abby's skin crawl. He locked eyes with Abby and then sniffed the air. His eyes and neck snapped toward Joe. An evil smile crept over his face as he stared at Joe. Alexander threw his head back and laughed. Flames surrounded him until he was completely gone.

Abby still stood just outside the fire. Small explosions kept happening inside, making the flames grow more. The firefighters were trying to keep all the members of the public back even though their eyes were still focused on the fire. People in the crowd were crying and discussing what they had just witnessed. Abby backed away from the fire and tried walking away. Joe went to join her, and people stared as they walked away from the flames. Joe's armor didn't help them look any less obvious. One of the firefighters ran over and tried asking questions. He was trying to act as an enforcer since the officers were gone.

Abby stopped and was prepared to tolerate him for a moment, but all three of them got distracted and looked around when they heard the moans of a man. Many of the buildings in Townsquare had their windows busted after the force of the explosion and much more damage, but the moans were coming from inside a building directly opposite from where the new city hall was.

Abby, Joe, and the firefighter walked over to take a look. The firefighter's questions were now on hold since his duty was calling him. The building was a small printing shop. The front glass was completely broken, making the whole shop easy to get into. Abby hopped over the broken glass and into the store.

"That's trespassing," the firefighter said, but it fell on deaf ears. Abby quickly saw who the injured person was—it was Chief Doyle. When she lost her cool and blasted him, he must have flown right across Townsquare and through the printing shop.

"Abby?" Chief Doyle said in a small, weak voice.

"It's you, you're back!" Abby said. The chief's eyes still had dark circles around them from being tired and injured, but the craziness and redness had went out of them. He had blisters forming on burns all over his body, and glass had cut up his head and arms so badly.

"I don't know what happened," the chief said. The firefighter got in and recognized the chief right away.

"Oy! Medical now!" the firefighter screamed at his partner. The second firefighter brought over a medical kit and stretcher, then went back to begin fighting the flames now that the small explosions inside had stopped.

"I can't take him until the fire is out," the firefighter said, grabbing the medical kit. "I can just try to make him stable, but there are no ambulances available." Abby looked back at the fire.

She had the ability to make fire appear but not the ability to make it stop. It would take hours to fight that fire. The chief didn't have hours.

"We'll take him," Abby said.

"Normally, I would go on about how that's against rules, but it could save his life," the firefighter replied.

"I'll go get the car," Joe said.

Abby tossed Joe the keys. He took out his sword and carefully stepped out of the printing shop. Abby stayed with Chief Doyle and helped the lone firefighter. She took the chief under his arms as gently as she could, and the firefighter grabbed his legs. They carefully placed him on the lowered stretcher. The chief yelled in pain.

"I don't understand how one of the fire victims even got over here," the firefighter said.

"I don't remember. I was at the station," Chief Doyle said, trying to remember why he was even there.

"Don't talk or stress yourself out right now," Abby said, trying to be as comforting as she knew how to be. Abby and the firefighter were startled by the sudden noise of a car skidding to a halt. Joe slammed the door hard and ran over to the smashed-in window. Abby and the firefighter raised the stretcher and carefully moved it to the door. Instead of climbing over broken glass and climbing out the window, they were taking the patient out the door. Chief Doyle was now out by the car.

"There's no way it's going to fit," Abby said, looking around at the small back seat, not knowing what to do.

"Here, we'll swap," the firefighter said, throwing his keys at Joe.

"All the equipment needed to fight the fire is in the truck," Joe said.

"Not that truck. I have a pickup parked at the fire station just a block over. Just leave the car there locked with the keys in it. I'll get it out and take it home until you return my truck," the firefighter said. Abby was shocked at the generous offer coming from someone they didn't even know. Joe hopped in the car and drove to the fire station without question.

"Are you sure about this?" Abby asked. "I know trucks are like a guy's baby."

The firefighter shook his head. "I wasn't expecting to find any more cops alive after we got the call about the explosion, let alone the chief. We're going to need him to rebuild after this is done," he said.

Abby smiled and placed her hand on his shoulder. It was refreshing to experience someone so optimistic, even under such terrible circumstances.

"What's your name?" the firefighter asked.

"Abby, and yours?"

"Rory," he said, holding out his hand to shake hers. Abby accepted although she was always worried about touching random people in case she burned them. They stopped shaking hands, but Rory didn't let go.

"There's something about your eyes," Rory said. Abby looked back at him but kept her distance. Trusting someone again wasn't on her mind right now.

Joe sped out of the side street and pulled up quickly. He jumped out of the truck.

"What did I interrupt here?" he said jokingly.

Abby took her hand away from Rory and placed it back on the stretcher. The pickup truck was black, and it had a cap on the back of it, closing in the entire back of the truck. Joe opened the truck and then walked over to help lift Chief Doyle into it. Abby put her bag in the front of the truck and opened it so Hecate could poke her head out. All three of them carefully lifted the chief into the back of the truck and closed him in there. Abby got into the passenger seat, and Joe jumped into the driver's seat. Rory hit the side of the truck twice before they sped off in the direction of the hospital.

The drive there was even more depressing than the reason they were going. The only people who were out were the people who were brave enough to go and see what the explosion was. Cars were still burning. After seeing how short-staffed the fire department was, it made sense that they were only focusing on the larger blazes. There were crazy-looking people standing outside with signs that read "The end of days are here" and other apocalypse-themed bullshit.

They approached the intersection, but they couldn't turn onto the main road leading to the hospital. A flaming ambulance was on its side along the road, blocking them. Abby got out of the passenger side and jumped off the pickup. She got closer to the ambulance until the flames were almost touching her. There were two paramedics dead in the front of the ambulance. Abby turned back around to tell Joe, but she saw a bunch of hooded figures approaching the truck. She looked at Joe and beckoned for him to come out. Joe stepped out of the truck and saw the figures.

"Get in the truck," Joe said. Abby looked back at the fire.

"The truck can't drive through it. We have to move it," Abby said. She kept running her hand through the flames like regular people do with water. It wasn't until recently that she realized how much stronger she felt near fire. It felt natural to her.

"Abby!" Joe yelled. But no one had a chance of getting close to her. She placed her hand in the fire again. Her whole body ignited, and her clothes started burning off. The fire ran through her body like a fast-moving river. Every single one of the hooded figures spontaneously burned into flames as she stared intensely at them. Their screams echoed throughout the street. Joe looked like he was watching in horror, but Abby didn't care. She still held the fire; her flaming hair blew in the wind, and her eyes glowed with evil as she watched them die. Her clothing had completely turned to ash now.

"Abby … we have to go," Joe said quietly, trying not to cause a battle between him and his fiery cousin. Abby took her hand out of the fire. Her hair and skin went back to normal before her eyes slowly did. It took her a moment to notice that she was standing there completely nude. Joe looked Abby up and down and then looked at his feet. Abby ran and got into the truck. Hecate was in the middle seat, still in the bag. The ambulance was now mostly melted by the temperatures Abby caused, and it seemed like they would be able to squeeze by if they went up on the sidewalk a little.

Joe kept looking at Abby's naked body and then out the window. He seemed unsure of how to react to his cousin's beauty or ashamed that he was having impure thoughts about her— thoughts that Rory the firefighter also shared.

Abby reached under the seat and found a Harmon City Fire sweater belonging to Rory. She stepped out of the truck and put it on. It barely covered past her ass, but at least it covered. She got back in the truck. Joe was completely red-faced.

"The clothes aren't fireproof," she said, trying to laugh it off and move on from the awkwardness. Joe turned on the car and smiled, trying not to be uncomfortable anymore. Abby opened the window to the back of the truck. "How are you doing back there, chief?" she asked loudly and got no response. "Hold on."

Joe put the truck back into park while Abby got out to check on the chief. She opened the back and climbed in. He was still breathing but no longer conscious. Abby closed the back of the truck with her still inside it. "Just go!" she said. Joe put the truck back into drive, and Abby held the stretcher as they bounced over the sidewalk, trying to get around the still-flaming ambulance.

"At least the ambulance shortage is explained," Joe said to himself while he drove. Abby heard him but didn't answer. Her focus was currently on the chief.

They had only been driving for a moment when Joe stopped again. "Hurry," he said to people outside the truck. A man and a woman jumped into the back of the truck. The woman was crying and holding her arm. It looked like a gunshot wound.

"We just drove through Townsquare an hour ago," the man said. "We didn't do anything, but our car was destroyed, and we were shot at. My wife was hit." The panic in the man's voice made it clear that they were both in shock.

"We're on our way to the hospital anyway," Abby said, still focusing on Chief Doyle.

"I don't know what we would have done if you guys didn't stop. I don't think we would have made it there. Our car was set on fire," he said. The man was in panic but was still holding his sobbing wife. Every time she saw the chief, she sobbed harder.

"He's not one of them," Abby said, trying to ease the woman's fears without giving her too much information and scaring her even more. Now that was a thin line.

"The police are crazy!" she yelled while still sobbing. Joe opened the windows separating the back cab of the truck and the front so he could hear what was happening.

"The police that attacked you guys are all dead," he said proudly. It seemed like Joe was hoping for that all along.

"Was that what the loud explosion was?" the man asked. His wife began to sob quieter. Abby hoped that meant she was stopping.

"Yeah, the whole city hall building is gone," Joe said. The woman began to sob again.

"Isn't that a good thing?" Abby asked, confused why she was still upset.

"She had just gotten an amazing new job there," the man replied.

"You guys just aren't having any luck, are you?" Joe joked, trying to lighten to mood.

11

The only good thing about Harmon being a dangerous town to go to was that it meant there weren't many cars on the road at all. The empty roads, combined with Joe's speed, meant it didn't take long for him to get to the hospital.

Abby got out, trying not to flash anyone in the process. She held the bottom of the sweater to keep it from riding up. The man helped his wife out of the truck, and they rushed into the hospital. Joe shut the truck off completely. He came around and started pulling the stretcher out. Abby reached out to help guide it down. Two males dressed in scrubs came out of the hospital to offer assistance. Once they saw that it was the chief of police, they eagerly got him into the hospital. A doctor ran to his side right away, and they took him away.

Since they were already at the hospital, Abby decided to go up and see how Ryan was doing. Joe still wasn't the biggest fan of

Ryan, so he offered to properly park the truck while she went up to see him. Abby agreed, and they walked away in opposite directions. Abby barely noticed all the looks she was getting because of how she was dressed. People's judgments didn't really work on Abby anymore.

Abby asked a nurse passing by if she knew what room Ryan was in. The nurse knew him right away, and Abby followed her directions. The hospital was so full. Patients were outside on stretchers in the halls. There were so many people yelling out in pain but not enough staff to tend to them all. You could tell who the people who had been evacuated to Harmon were; their suitcases were packed and all over the halls too.

Abby finally got to Ryan's room. She looked through the small window. He was laughing and watching television. A nurse was talking to him, and he seemed to be his old kind self again. The nurse came out the door, and Abby stood out of the way.

"Can I help you, ma'am?" the nurse asked, looking at Abby with suspicion.

"No, wrong room," Abby said. She got away from his room as quickly as possible. Abby rushed back down to meet Joe, but instead, she ran into him while she was leaving.

"That was a short visit," Joe commented.

"I couldn't go in," she replied. She continued walking down the hall. Abby and Joe took a seat in the small lounge that was just inside the hospital's lobby. They looked at each other in the reflection on the glass separating them from the outside.

"If Alexander can affect the people around him, does that mean I can too?" Abby asked.

"I would assume so, but you don't seem like you would be doing it willingly," Joe replied.

Abby put her head in her hands for a second. "It's not. But Ryan is perfectly normal now that he's been away from me," Abby said. Joe nodded in agreement.

"I sensed something was changing in him when I first met him. I thought it was Alexander, but this makes more sense," Joe replied. Abby didn't like the idea of having to stay away from Ryan. She was okay with not being around other people for long lengths of time. She just missed the Ryan she originally met.

"I just miss how good things were since the end of winter," Abby said. Joe put his hand on Abby's arm.

"Let's just rest here for a while. I'll go get us some coffee and put this armor in the truck. We can wait to see how your chief friend is," Joe replied. Abby nodded in agreement, and Joe got up. He went outside first and got rid of the armor. Once Abby found pants, the two of them would almost look normal again. Joe came back in and walked to a small café in the corner of the main level.

Abby sat alone for a few minutes. She looked through the glass to the parking lot of the hospital. People were still being brought in by ambulances that looked like they were from outside towns despite the storms all moving toward the city of Harmon. People came in talking about how the storms had badly damaged their homes. Abby listened as a group of people reunited with the other half of their family. Joe got back with the coffees and handed Abby one with two creams in it.

"How did you know what I take in my coffee?" Abby asked.

"I listen," Joe said proudly. Abby took a sip and looked back outside.

"Do you think this city will ever get back to normal again?" Abby asked randomly as she looked at the panic on some people's faces.

"I think so. I mean, it happened before when no one thought it would. So who's to say it can't happen again?" Joe said back to Abby. Abby wanted to believe that as well, but she was worried that this was Harmon's one chance to bounce back, and she blew it.

"Are you sure you don't want to go visit Ryan?" Joe asked. Abby paused for a moment.

"Yes," she said bluntly.

"You two seemed close. Are you sure that staying away is really what you want?" Joe asked.

Abby wasn't ever sure about what she wanted other than peace and solidarity, but it didn't seem like that was something she could ever get. "I think I need to stay far away from people. If I spend any large amount of time with them, then they'll just start changing like he did," Abby said, referring to Ryan's new dark personality whenever he's around her.

"Maybe there's a way to stop it," Joe suggested. Abby shook her head.

"I can't stop doing something that I have no control over. It's just best for me to keep my distance, especially now that Ryan is one of the very few cops left alive in the city," Abby said.

"I could stay with you," Joe blurted out. Abby looked at him in confusion.

"It's good to have at least one person you can rely on, and your evil presence wouldn't affect me since we're blood relatives,"

Joe said, making a very reasonable point. Abby wasn't not considering it, but in the back of her mind, she wanted to just take Hecate, find her hellhounds, and run far away alone. Finding a cousin was never part of the fantasy.

"Let's just see if Alexander leaves us alive long enough to plan a future," Abby replied.

As Joe and Abby sat and talked, now and then Abby would feel Joe going inside her head. He didn't seem like he was good at reading people, so she just figured he wanted to know what she was thinking about him. Joe didn't seem like the kind of guy who was into impressing people, but it seemed like he was both excited and intrigued to know he had family around, especially family who wasn't trying to kill him.

"So did you really have hellhounds on earth?" Joe asked. Abby smiled and nodded.

"You should have met them. They were so beautiful," Abby said.

"They would have probably tried to kill me. Their hate for my father might pass on to me," he explained.

"Oh, maybe it's best you didn't meet them," Abby joked.

They both looked outside. A man dressed in a blue golf shirt walked in, and Joe got up and went to meet him. Abby looked on, confused, until Joe handed him money and started carrying a pizza box back to where Abby was still sitting.

"You ordered pizza to a hospital?" Abby laughed. Joe looked around at the few people looking at them.

"Yeah, is that weird?" he asked.

"Just open it. I'm so damn hungry," she said.

He opened it. It was a large, plain cheese pizza. Abby took a slice. She wanted to comment about how they liked the same boring cheese pizza, but she kept quiet. Joe was already feeling connected to her, and she wasn't even sure if she would be alive long enough to feel as connected to him. With Alexander on the loose, life wasn't certain for anyone, especially Abby.

As time passed while they chatted, night rolled in again. It got darker outside than Abby had every seen it before. The night falling over them combined with the storms approaching from all directions made it look like a blackout.

"With how dark it is right now, it would be a perfect time for Alexander to cause some crap and run about unseen," Joe said, looking out the glass into the darkness.

"He already runs around unseen and causing shit in the daylight," Abby said. Joe got up and looked through the glass closer.

"If it gets any darker, he could be standing a few feet from us and we wouldn't know," Joe said.

"I'd know it. I'd sense it," Abby said. She got up and stood beside Joe. "Are you afraid of the dark?" she asked jokingly. Their joking was cut short when a young nurse called out Abby's name.

"That's me!" Abby yelled, turning around to face the nurse.

"Charles Doyle is stable and asked to see you," the young nurse said.

"Okay, where is he?" Abby asked.

The nurse pointed. "It's straight down this hall past the washrooms, and then it's the first door on the right," the nurse said.

Abby waited a moment for Joe to join her. He was throwing away the empty pizza box from earlier. They walked down the hall together.

"Did we demolish that whole pizza?" Abby asked.

"We sure did," Joe said, putting his hand up to his mouth before quietly burping.

Abby got to the chief's door and looked in before entering. His body was completely bandaged up, and only a small portion of his face was left free. That part of his face was cut and burnt as well.

Another nurse squeezed past them to check on Chief Doyle. After she checked all his readings, she began putting ointment on the exposed facial wounds. She was quick about it, knowing that visitors were waiting outside his room. Once she was done, the nurse told her to go ahead in. The nurse looked Abby up and down, likely wondering why she was only wearing a sweater. It was still a little shocking that no one had offered her pants yet. Abby walked in slowly.

Joe whispered to her, "I'm going to wait in the truck. He doesn't know me, and it might just stress him out." He was trying to consider the patient's feelings.

"Thank you," Abby said, smiling back at Joe.

"Take as long as you want. I'll be napping," Joe said as he walked out the door.

Abby walked over to the chief's bedside. He strained his eyes and looked up at her. "You look all mummified," Abby said, trying to lighten the mood. His injuries looked so severe.

"They won't tell me what happened," Chief Doyle said weakly. Abby wasn't sure if the doctors simply didn't want to upset him by telling him as much as they knew or if the doctors just had no idea.

"What's the last thing you remember?" Abby asked. Chief Doyle closed his eyes, his face strained.

"We got him. Three squad cars showed up, and a few officers brought him into the station," the chief said. Then he paused, not sure what to say next.

"And then what?" Abby asked, trying not to press too hard.

"I don't know. I remember lying on the ground in unbearable pain," he replied. His heart monitor showed his heart racing as he got emotional, trying to understand. Abby sighed and pulled a chair over to the side of the bed. She sat down, unsure of how to explain what happened.

"Alexander and myself have this curse about us, it seems," Abby tried explaining. Chief Doyle looked confused, but not in disbelief. With everything that's happened to and around him, there would be no reason for him to question odd happenings anymore.

"A curse?" he asked, trying to understand.

"It's mild with me, but when I'm around someone for too long, they start to take on the worst traits of my personality. It's like they turn a little evil," she explained. The chief looked like he finally got some information he could process and understand.

"So the change in Ryan's personality and his violence on the job was you?" the chief asked.

"Yes, but I didn't know it was happening. I've never been that close to someone before," Abby said, trying to make herself sound a little less responsible for the mayhem. The chief waited a moment before answering.

"Why didn't it affect me when you were around me?" he asked.

"I only came to the station for a few minutes here and there. I don't think there was enough time for it to happen," she said.

Chief Doyle was asked her these questions as though she were an expert on this, but really she was just as clueless as he was on this issue. After the chief had a few minutes to think, he came back with even more questions.

"Where's Ryan?" he asked.

"He's actually in the hospital as well. He's doing great though," she answered.

"So Alexander influenced us and that's why I don't remember?" the chief asked. Abby nodded. "But I barely remember him being locked in the holding cell before it went blank. Why did he affect us so quickly when it takes you a while?" he asked.

Finally, a good question that even had Abby stomped. "That, I can't answer. I think he may have a way to control it, but I don't understand how," Abby said.

The chief tried sitting up a bit on the bed. Abby helped by pressing a button on the side of the bed that lifted the head portion up a bit. He looked down at his body covered with bandages.

"This is another thing I don't understand. They said there was an explosion and I was found a safe distance away from it, yet I'm covered in burns like I was right beside the explosion," he said.

Abby looked at him and down at her feet. "I'm not sure about that," she answered. She wasn't happy with herself for lying to the chief, but knowing that she was the one who burned him so badly wouldn't help anyone right now.

"Who else was injured during this explosion? Any other officers?" the chief asked. Now he was getting into territory that would definitely upset him.

"Why don't we wait to talk about that?" Abby said. The chief looked angry—at least from what Abby could tell by the tiny amount of his face showing.

"Everyone keeps saying that. The doctors and nurses are cowards. Now tell me the damn truth," the chief demanded. Abby knew it was a serious moment, but she couldn't help but feel a bit amused by the bandaged chief trying to yell. *If I wasn't going to hell before, I definitely will now,* she thought.

"Okay, if you really need to know, I'll tell you exactly what happened. But it's going to hurt you, and you'll probably hate me afterward," Abby said, hoping her words would make the chief rethink what he wanted to know. Sometimes knowing doesn't make you better; it makes you much worse off than you were before.

"I need to know," he said firmly.

Abby took a breath before beginning. She was hoping the chief would be able to think clearly but knew he wouldn't because of the obvious blinding pain he was in. A nurse came in just as she was about to begin and started another morphine drip for Chief Doyle. She looked at Abby awkwardly for not having pants on and left. Abby rolled her eyes and started.

"I don't know when he corrupted you and your officers exactly, but you all came to my apartment under the tunnels. Me and

Ryan were leaving and noticed you were trying to unseal the entrance that you just ordered sealed a few months ago," Abby said.

The chief cut in. "But I would never do that," he said in a shocked voice.

"You obviously wouldn't tell your officers to fire on sight at us, but you did. Me and Ryan ended up trapping you down in the tunnels for a little while. But you somehow got out. My guess is, Alexander let you out. And then the story gets even worse," Abby continued. The chief looked in terror, waiting to find out what had happened.

"Under Alexander's trance, you took over Townsquare and shot anyone who tried to pass through. We decided that getting captured would likely lead us to Alexander, but instead he made you guys ..." Abby trailed off, not wanting to continue.

"He made us what?" the chief asked roughly.

"He made you blow up the new city hall building. The goal was to do it with me inside. The back door was completely blocked by the officers, and you were at the front. You fired one round, and I fired back," Abby said, looking over the bandages covering the damage her reaction caused.

"I'm so sorry. Joe got hit and went down, and I did the only thing my instincts allowed in order to defend ourselves from you. You weren't yourself at all," Abby said.

The chief's eyes watered up a tiny bit. He strained his face trying to act normal and fight off any tears. He didn't seem like a man who cried in front of anyone easily. Abby hoped she had answered the questions properly and that being truthful in that moment was a good idea.

The chief looked like he had more questions, but the morphine started kicking in. His eyes were closing even though he was trying to fight it. It only took a moment before they didn't open again, and he was resting.

12

*A*bby sat by Chief Doyle's bed for a while, waiting to see if he was going to wake up anytime soon with more questions. She also figured it would be good for him to wake up and see a familiar face, although she wasn't sure if her face would be very calming for him. Since Abby was introduced into the chief's life, it had been nothing but complete chaos. Sometimes Abby had no idea why he was still so kind to her—in his normal state of mind, of course.

Abby's thoughts were interrupted when she heard steps coming in the door behind her. She turned around and looked to see who was there, expecting it to be another nurse. It was Rory, the firefighter whose truck they had borrowed.

"Hey," he said softly.

"Hey," Abby replied.

"We were just wondering how he's doing," Rory said.

"We?" Abby asked.

"My partner. He's just taking our work truck back to the station, then meeting me here," Rory explained. He walked into the room from the doorway and looked at Chief Doyle.

"He's stable, but it's pretty serious, as you can see," Abby said, looking back over at the chief.

"Has he been out for long?" Rory asked.

Abby shook her head. "I think he'll be out for a while. They started his morphine drip not too long ago," Abby said.

"Why don't we talk outside?" Rory suggested, trying not to bother the chief.

"Okay," Abby said.

She got up and followed Rory, who was already walking out the door. He went into a small room just a bit further down the hall. Abby walked behind him. There was no one else in there even though the hospital was so busy. That's how small and unknown this tiny waiting room was. She closed the door behind them so they could talk in private. Abby figured it was more questions about the chief. Rory turned around and looked at Abby. In the hospital room, she was sitting on the chair in a way that he wouldn't see the front of her.

"Is that my sweater?" he asked as his face went redder by the second.

"Yes, I'm really sorry. It was an emergency. I would give it back now, but I haven't had time to grab something else to throw on," she explained.

"So you're not even wearing pants?" he asked slowly.

"No, it's pretty breezy," she joked awkwardly. Rory stuttered a bit and went quiet, his hands fidgeting. Abby waited for a moment while Rory stared at her.

"What is it you wanted to talk about?" she asked, trying not to make him more uncomfortable. Rory gulped and cleared his throat.

"The chief and stuff," he said, stumbling for words.

"I'm sure you'll be able to talk to him soon," Abby said, unsure of what she could share with Rory. Abby sat down beside Rory. He moved a little and kept fidgeting with his hands on his lap. Someone opened the door and quickly apologized before closing it.

"That was weird," Rory said, trying to act normal. Through the open door, Abby saw an open storage closet.

"Hold on, I might be able to grab something," she said. She got up and felt the breeze on her butt. She rushed to the door, hoping she didn't completely moon Rory. She went outside the waiting room they were talking in and slipped into the storage closet while no one was looking. She closed the door behind her and started looking through a rack of scrubs for a pair of pants her size or with a drawstring. Just as she reached up on the top shelf, exposing her entire naked bottom half, Rory walked in. He had followed her across the hall, looking to see if she needed help.

"Oh, wow," he said. He tried to look away but just kept staring. Abby realized what had happened and quickly put her arms down, covering herself again. She turned around and dropped the scrub pants she had found.

"Close the door," she said quickly, hoping he didn't just attract attention to them in the closet. Rory listened and reached to close the door without taking his eyes off her.

"What?" she said, looking back at Rory, who was staring at her. It was impossible not to notice the rapid rise happening in the front of his pants.

"I'm sorry, I've just never had a beautiful woman wear my clothes before, especially one that I just saw that much of," he admitted. He walked a bit closer to Abby, and she took a step back until she was against the shelf with the scrubs.

"I'm sorry," he said, backing away. "I've just been working so much with everything that's happening in the city I haven't even seen a beautiful woman naked, let alone touched one in a long time." His face was completely red now. Abby tried to see in his head when he stepped toward her, but he didn't have an evil thought at all. Part of her was thinking he was another one of Alexander's trance victims.

"It's been a while for me too," Abby said, trying to make him feel better. It wasn't a complete lie. It's been a long time since she was touched softly and since she felt that fulfilling sense of pleasure. Ryan had been so rough lately that he rarely even cared about her pleasure. He mostly just took what he wanted and went to sleep.

Abby moved forward until she was against Rory. She put her arms around his neck, not caring about the sweater riding up and revealing herself again. She placed her lips on his, and they kissed passionately. His hands ran down her waist until it touched her bare ass cheeks. His hands wandered between her legs. He rubbed her gently before slowly slipping one finger between her lips. His finger gently brushed against her clit before wandering down and stopping at the opening of her vagina. He traced around it. Abby tightened her legs a bit.

"Are you sure this is the time for something like this?" Abby asked, trying to be reasonable even though it was hard for her to fight these strong urges.

"It won't take that long, believe me," Rory joked. They both giggled a bit. Rory took his hands away from Abby and locked the door. He turned back around and pulled Abby to him. Abby knew this wasn't the time or place, but she couldn't see Ryan anymore, and she had to take care of these urges somehow.

They started making out hard, and Rory's breathing got heavier as Abby reached down and undid his pants. It fell down a tiny bit, and she tugged at his boxers to come off his hips. His cock was completely hard and already starting to ooze cum. He was fairly long but thick as hell. Abby rubbed his massive hard-on against her clit as they stood in the closet making out. Rory lifted her up, and Abby wrapped her legs around his waist. He pushed Abby against the wall. The motion and the force made his cock enter her without warning. She gasped.

He started pumping slowly but got faster and faster the more excited he got. Abby closed her eyes and put her head against the wall she was being forced into. She moaned quietly as she got wetter and wetter. He fucked her against the wall for only about a minute until he groaned loudly and began shaking a bit. He held on to Abby's waist, holding her in place as his hips buckled involuntarily while he finished. They both tried to stay quiet for a minute in case someone had heard Rory's loud finish.

"Holy shit," he said. Rory's hands went from Abby's waist and slowly up his sweater until he was groping her boobs. He stood there for a while just touching her and twitching as he pumped his load deep inside her. He stood there with Abby still against the wall for a couple of minutes, not wanting to pull out of her.

"I should put pants on soon and find somewhere to clean up," Abby said, trying to hold on.

"Didn't you have a bag with you at Townsquare?" Rory asked, out of breath.

"Yeah, I have a tank top in it but no pants," she replied. Abby waited for a moment. "Am I coming down sometime soon?" she asked with a laugh. She was still impaled against the wall.

"Yeah, sorry. I wanted to make it last but failed during it," he said with a nervous laugh.

"It was great," Abby said as he slowly put her down. He gently pulled himself out of her, and cum dripped down her bare legs. Abby grabbed a towel off a shelf in the closet and wiped herself down. Abby threw the cum-stained towel in a small garbage can just inside the door they locked. She put on the scrub pants she had dropped when things got heated and ran her fingers through her hair. Rory slowly did his pants back up.

"I can't believe that just happened," he kept saying over and over.

Abby and Rory peeked out of the closet, making sure no one was looking when they came out.

"Is your partner bringing the car here? We could just exchange it here to make things easier," Abby suggested.

"Yeah, that works," he said, still trying to catch his breath.

"Want to go outside then?" Abby said, trying to get Rory to follow. He did, and they walked quickly out of the hospital. The air was a lot colder now that night had rolled in, and after that heated moment, they both needed to cool off.

"Do you see your truck anywhere?" Abby asked. Rory looked around until he saw his black pickup in a corner spot near the road. He pointed to the truck and finished fiddling with his pants. They walked across the parking lot toward it.

"Joe, the guy I was with when we met in Townsquare, is probably sleeping in it by now," she said. Rory rolled his eyes and looked disappointed.

"Oh crap, he's not your boyfriend or something, is he?" he asked. It seemed like it wouldn't be the first time for him to get that crappy news after being with a girl.

"No, my cousin. I don't have a boyfriend anymore," she said. Rory stopped when they got to the truck.

"Are you looking for one?" he asked awkwardly. Abby laughed, not sure how to answer that.

"Um, I really can't have anything long-term," she said, trying to be as vague as possible.

"Hey!" said a loud, drowsy voice. Joe got out of the truck and came around to the passenger side where they were standing. Abby smiled at Joe for unknowingly saving her from this awkward conversation.

"What's going on over here?" he said, looking at the pair.

"Where's my bag and Hecate?" Abby asked, ignoring Joe's awkward question.

"Right inside there," he said, pointing to the passenger door. Abby opened the door. Rory looked intrigued.

"What's a Hecate?" he asked. Abby opened the backpack completely and picked up her cat, who was very happy to see her.

149

"This is a Hecate," she said, smiling. Hecate pawed out at Rory as he went to pet her. Abby set her down on the seat and grabbed a black tank top from a side pocket of the bag. Just then, Rory's partner pulled in with Ryan's car and parked it behind Joe's truck. He shook both Joe's and Abby's hands and introduced himself, but Abby was so distracted that she forgot his name right away. That happened a lot to her actually. She looked back at the car in confusion.

"I quickly replaced the windshield for you guys," said Rory's partner.

"Wow, thank you," Abby said.

"Don't mention it. You guys saved the chief!" he replied. Rory looked at his partner and back to Abby. His partner looked at both of them like he knew something had happened between them.

"Don't look," Abby said. She turned around and took off Rory's sweater and quickly put on the tank top in her hand. She turned around, and all three guys were staring at her, shocked.

"Oh please," she said, throwing Rory's sweater back at him. Rory smelled the sweater automatically. Joe looked at him in disgust and confusion.

"We're wanted back at the station," Rory's partner said, looking at him with the same confused and grossed-out face after seeing that. Without thinking, Rory leaned in and hugged Abby deeply, burying his face in her neck. He let her go, and she grabbed her bag. Hecate was already sitting in it again, so she just carried her inside it to Ryan's car. Rory's partner got in the passenger side of the truck where Hecate had been. Abby leaned into the back of the car and put Hecate in. She turned around and got in the passenger side since Joe had already put a few of his things in the driver's side, making it clear he was driving. Rory waited to get into the driver's side of his truck and kept looking at Abby while Joe finished packing his armor and weapons away in the trunk again. Joe got in and turned the car on. Rory smiled and waved goodbye. Abby smile back at him as they started driving away.

They drove in silence while they exited the parking lot. Abby could tell that Joe wanted to say something, but he would be walking on eggshells. He finally asked quietly, "Did something happen between you and that firefighter?"

Abby grinned and looked at him. "Oh yeah," she said, smiling.

"What happened?" he asked.

Abby laughed. "You want details? He got horny, I'm always horny, and I didn't have pants. What do you think happened?" Abby said bluntly.

Joe smiled and laughed. "I can't believe you fucked a firefighter in the hospital," he said, laughing his ass off. Abby laughed along with him.

"At least I burned all those pizza calories off," she said, fueling more laughter between the pair. They drove for a while, laughing and making jokes.

"I just realized we have no idea where we're going," Joe said. Abby looked around.

"That's true," she said, thinking about it. There were no other leads to where Alexander was at that moment. She thought it was likely that he was in the tunnels near her place, but even that wasn't certain.

"We should go back to my place, freshen up, and see what the news are saying now," Joe said.

Abby nodded. "That makes sense," she said, impressed that he was thinking so strategically right now.

"Just one question, though," Joe said. Abby looked at him, waiting for it. "If you're no longer able to be with Ryan anymore, then should we be using his car?" Joe asked.

Abby thought for a moment. "It's fine. I'll leave it parked at the building for when he gets home."

They drove quickly through the dark streets back to Joe's building. The sky was so dark that Abby couldn't tell the difference between the dark sky and the crazy storm moving toward Harmon. There were next to no cars on the road, and barely any people except the crazies were out on the streets. They pulled into the parking lot to Joe's building and sat there a moment.

"That was a hell of a day," Joe said, taking off his seat belt and sitting back in his seat.

"And it's not over yet," Abby added.

C H A P T E R

13

Joe and Abby walked into the building. Abby held the bag holding Hecate in her arms. As soon as they got to the door, they both looked at each other, sensing that something wasn't right. Joe went to put his key in the door's lock, but the slightest touch nudged it open. Joe walked in first with his sword drawn. No one was there, but they could still sense he was near. Joe looked at his old books with the details of their bloodline; they were opened and tossed around.

"I think we just missed Alexander," Joe said, looking at a specific book that was open. The book told stories of how the devil would return to earth. One of the stories on the page detailed how the devil was already walking among us but was only in mortal form with limited abilities until the gates of hell were unlocked. Abby and Joe both read the passage and looked at each other in confusion and worry.

"So he wants to unlock the gates of hell? What does that even mean?" Joe said. Abby grabbed the book from Joe and read it again.

"I don't think we want to find out," Abby said, closing the book and putting it back in her bag.

"Why are you taking it?" Joe asked.

"Alexander knows where you live and who you are. This isn't safe anymore," Abby said. Joe put his hands on his head, not knowing what to grab first. He got a garbage bag from his kitchen and began filling it with blankets and items they may need. Abby put Hecate on the couch while they packed. She grabbed a few more books that seemed to have interested Alexander so she could study them to see if there was a way she could reverse his damage.

When Joe thought Abby wasn't looking, he snuck some weed and a small pipe into his pocket.

"Do you really need that?" Abby asked, turning around and looking at Joe.

"Right now, more than you know actually," he said, sitting down for a moment and picking up his bong.

"We don't have time for this. It isn't safe here," Abby said, trying to rush her cousin. Joe ignored her and took a deep breath, inhaling a crazy amount of smoke.

"Don't forget to grab munchies," he said, ignoring Abby's concern. Abby shook her head at Joe and kept grabbing things she may need.

"I wish I could go back to my place again," she said.

"You never did say where that was," Joe said once he stopped coughing. Abby made a deal with the chief never to tell anyone that she was living down there. That was the only thing stopping her, until now. After all, it's not like she could go back there anytime soon.

"I lived under Townsquare," Abby said.

Joe looked shocked. "Like, where Alexander lived?" he asked. Alexander lingering in the tunnels under the city had been all over the news. People felt so unsafe knowing someone that evil had been just under their feet all along.

"Not exactly. It was even farther underground than the tunnels. That's where me, Hecate, and the hounds stayed," she explained.

"And Ryan?" Joe asked. Abby rolled her eyes.

"And Ryan a lot of the time," she said, remembering that was in the past now.

"Have you thought about what you're going to tell him?" Joe asked regarding Abby's relationship with Ryan.

"Honestly, I've been thinking about just disappearing," she admitted. "Once Alexander is gone, Harmon needs to get back to a normal-functioning city. I don't think my presence will help that at all."

Joe laughed and got up from the couch. Hecate purred, looking up at them.

"Sometimes you sound like the opposite of evil," Joe said jokingly. *Good,* Abby thought. The hate she had for her own bloodline made it easier for her to fight against her natural evil instincts.

Joe put on the TV for a minute and switched it to the news channel. There were no reporters on the air. Everyone had been sent home, and there was just a warning message across the screen to stay indoors due to an escaped prisoner and the unexplained weather approaching. Abby and Joe looked at each other as he turned the TV off and tossed the remote down on the couch. The city of Harmon was getting worse and worse every minute Alexander was on the loose.

Joe tugged his bag full of items out the door. Abby put her filled backpack on her back and held Hecate in her arms. No one was in the halls at all anymore. Abby and Joe had to walk by the main front doors in order to get to the side doors leading to the parking lot. Someone had chained the main doors shut to ensure no one unwanted would get inside. When they got outside, they waited besides the building and looked around before going out into the open parking lot.

"The calm before the storm," Joe said, looking around. It was silent. There were no screams, gunshots, or fighting—nothing. Even the wind seemed to be absent. It was almost creepy how silent it was. Abby and Joe crept out to the car quickly. Abby put her bag and Hecate in the back, and Joe threw his garbage bag full of stuff with his armor in the trunk. Abby got in the passenger side and waited for Joe.

"Are you sure it's okay to take his car again?" Joe asked, referring to Ryan. Abby gave him an odd look; there were more important things to worry about than using someone's car too much.

"The hospital said they were keeping him for observation for a couple days. We've got a while," Abby said. Joe started the car and drove out of the lot, looking back once at the building he may not return to.

"Did you grab everything related to you and your dad?" Abby asked. Joe nodded. The last thing they needed was someone getting ahold of information about them. Then they would definitely have to leave town and just let Harmon go. Abby used to like living in Harmon, but now there was way too much work to keep it safe.

"I think I've made up my mind," Abby said out loud.

"About what?" Joe asked, not taking his eyes off the road in case there were dangers up ahead.

"I need to leave Harmon," she said.

"Where would you go?" Joe asked. Abby looked out the window into the dark night.

"Anywhere but nowhere too long," she said confusingly.

"So you're just going to be a drifter?" Joe laughed. Abby chuckled but wasn't turned off by the idea. It seemed like wherever she decided to call home would always be taken away from her anyway.

Abby looked in the back seat. Hecate was curled up sleeping and using Abby's bag as a pillow.

"I keep getting in this car and driving even though I have no idea where we're going," Joe complained.

Abby knew that they didn't have time to screw around, but they were also half mortal. They needed a safe place to stop, rest, and eat. Abby also needed a while in peace in order to read through all the books from Joe's place that Alexander was so interested in.

"There's a place just outside town. It's a small cabin. It should still be abandoned," Abby said, trying to remember exactly where the small structure was that she and Ryan hid in during the winter.

"Okay, which way?" Joe asked.

"Just keep going straight on the main road until we hit the edge of town, then there's a long, narrow driveway," Abby said, giving vague instructions because she had forgotten the address. Joe had no other options, so he accepted the crappy instructions and drove as fast as he could out of town without attracting attention to themselves. The closer they got to the edge of Harmon, the darker it got. The storms were moving slowly toward them from all directions. They both looked up at the sky.

"Part of me wants to know what will happen when the storms all meet together over the top of Harmon," Joe said.

"Why don't you suffocate that part of yourself?" Abby snapped back. Joe laughed it off. He had smoked so much weed at the house that insults meant nothing to him. The storms were so close now; it looked like they were closing in on Harmon.

Joe drove to the outskirts of town, and Abby pointed to the narrow driveway. They drove into it. The cabin wasn't there anymore; now on that land stood a trailer with an older settle man sitting in front of it. The man was reading until the couple drove up. He looked up from his book and waved at Abby and Joe.

"It was a cabin," Abby said. Joe looked around at the emptiness other than the trailer.

"It's still a good place to relax if we can get that guy out of here," Joe said. Abby was hoping Joe wasn't talking about getting rid of the older man and taking his home.

"He might be cool," Abby said, trying to be positive. Deep down, she was just hoping that he wasn't another crazy person they would have to get rid of. Abby got out of the car first.

"Hey there," the older man said loudly. He seemed friendly enough. Joe got out of the car, and the man got up and went inside, still with a smile on his face.

"Is that a bad sign?" Joe said. He kept his hand on the door of the car in case he needed to quickly grab his sword. Abby stepped closer to the trailer. It was small and white with some discoloration from the sun. There was a very old BBQ off to the side with something cooking inside it. The man burst out the door to his trailer home, making Abby jump back.

"Coffee?" the man loudly offered, unaware of their suspicion. Abby sensed no evil around him and knew it was safe, but she still didn't understand why he was out here alone.

"Thank you," Abby said, accepting an aged mug from the man. Joe was still standing by the car. The man held up another mug to show Joe and set it on a small plastic table near the book he was reading.

"Here," the man said, handing Abby a foldout lawn chair.

"Reminds me of your living room furniture," Abby said, looking back at Joe. Hecate jumped on the dashboard of the car.

"And who's that?" the man asked, smiling at the glowing eyes coming from the car. Joe opened up the door and brought Hecate out. The darkness almost made her invisible other than her bright eyes.

"I have something for you too," the kind man said to Hecate before petting her. He got up once again and went inside.

"What's his deal?" Joe asked.

"What do you mean?" Abby said, confused.

"He's being nice—almost too nice," Joe said.

The man came out holding a dish. Abby was expecting it to be filled with milk or something, but it was actually a dish of wet cat food. Hecate buried her face in it.

"Do you have a cat?" Abby asked, wondering why a single man would travel around with cat food.

"He was my late wife's. He just died last week. Twenty-three—damn good age for a cat," he said. The man offered Joe and Abby cream and sugar for their coffees.

The three sat down by the table outside the trailer. They were surrounded by fields. Harmon was just off in the distance.

"What happened to the cabin that was here?" Abby asked. The man got up and checked on his BBQ. He flipped over some burgers that were on the grill and put a couple more on.

"That cabin burned down in the winter," the man said as he walked back over to take a seat. "I'm Albert, but everyone calls me Al. Or they did anyway," he said, extending his hand out to shake Joe's. Abby took a drink of her coffee. It wasn't the best coffee she had tasted, but then again, it wasn't the worst.

"I'm Joe. This is my cousin, Abby," he said, trying to make small talk with the man.

"Oh, I thought you two were a couple," Al said. Joe laughed and shook his head.

"No, she was dating a cop for a while," Joe said, opening up to Al. Abby looked away and remembered the amazing moments she and Ryan shared alone in that cabin. "Now it seems like she's moved on to firefighters," Joe joked, referring to her encounter with Rory. Abby shot Joe a look.

"Why are you out here all alone, Al?" Abby said, trying to change the subject from her chaotic love life. Al looked a little uncomfortable with the question.

"Well, why are you guys out here?" he said, finally asking the question that Abby was expecting him to ask in the first place.

"We're looking for a safe place to spend a few hours," Abby said, trying to give as little information as possible to the friendly stranger.

"Well, that's why I'm here. I've lost everyone in that hell of a city you call Harmon. I hate that place," the man said. This was the first time he seemed less than friendly. There was still no evil running through him though; it just seemed like his anger toward the city was fueled by his pain and grief.

"I'm sorry for your loss," Joe said, trying to be comforting. He was almost as bad as Abby when it came to relating to people's emotions.

"Losses," Al said, correcting Joe. Al reached into his jacket pocket and pulled out an old brown leather wallet. He took out a photo and handed it to Abby. It was a picture of him, looking not much different than he did now, with an older woman and a young couple. "That's my wife. Her name was Lorna," Al said, tracing the woman's face fondly. "And that's my son and daughter-in-law." He pointed to each individual in the picture as he described them.

"Are they all gone?" Joe asked. He immediately looked at his feet, feeling awkward about the weight of that question he asked a stranger. The man's eyes filled with tears and got heavy.

"My wife was gunned down in the winter, and my son was a police officer. He went missing after killing his wife two days ago. She was pregnant with my grandchild," the man said. Abby looked at Joe. There wasn't a chance that his son wasn't dead; he was definitely gone. Abby touched the man's hand to try and comfort him. The man wiped away his tears and got up, going over to the BBQ again.

"What do you two take on your burgers?" he asked, trying to sound upbeat again even though his heartache was breaking through the wall of strength he was trying to display.

"Just a bit of ketchup," Abby said awkwardly.

"Same," Joe said, unsure of what to say after his last question blew up so badly. Albert put some buns on the grill to toast them and sat back down for a moment. They all looked down at Hecate, who was still trying to finish the huge pile of cat food on her plate.

"You can stay here tonight. I don't have room in the trailer, but I have a tent you guys can put up to get some sleep," Albert said.

"Thank you. I could definitely sleep," Joe said, trying to be friendly to the broken man. Albert got up and fixed the burgers. He brought them over on a large plate. All of them had just ketchup on them, so they all picked one and ate. Abby wasn't very hungry after all the pizza she and Joe had eaten just a few hours before, but she accepted Albert's generous offer and ate as much as she could. She was more grateful for the coffee that he brought for them.

14

The fire cracked loudly. It was the only thing that made noise in that area other than themselves. Abby and Joe still sat at the table, while Albert quickly started a fire by himself. Abby was impressed, even though she could have gotten it done even faster.

Joe and Abby got up and joined Albert to sit around the fire. The light really helped see the expressions on one another's faces. The small light on the outside of the trailer above the table they were sitting at before didn't help at all. The heat coming from the fire was nice for Abby too. Although she was naturally hot, the cold night air combined with how exhausted she was gave her a chill. It didn't help that she had burned up the clothing she was in and was only wearing a tank top and a thin pair of nurse's scrubs—uncomfortable nurse's scrubs too. Abby tugged at them to try and gain comfort.

"So are you a nurse?" Al asked, looking at Abby's pants.

"No, I just had to borrow these," Abby said. Borrowing implied she had the intention to give them back, but she intended to throw the uncomfortable things in the garbage when she was done with them. It went quiet for a moment. "How do you stay so positive after all that's happened?" Abby asked. She wasn't sure if it was the right moment, but she just had to know. To her, remaining positive throughout horrors in life was a superpower that she just couldn't possess.

Albert smiled at Abby. "Look at me. I'm old. I'll be with them soon enough. Besides, Lorna would be furious with me if I acted any less than what I am," Albert said, smiling.

"She sounds amazing," Abby said.

"Oh, she was. She was something special," Al said.

"Was it Alexander?" Joe asked with immediate regret. Abby looked at Joe with her mouth open. Albert got visibly upset.

"How dare you say that name here!" Al said angrily. Hecate got up on Al's lap and lay down in a quick attempt to be calming. Al started petting her, and she began to purr. It was a small action, but it was enough to smooth out the tension.

"I'm sorry," Joe said, but Abby put up her hand to tell him to shut up. Abby wasn't sure what to say in order to smooth things over, but she was sure that they needed to stay there for the night. It was the only safe place that she could think of.

"We've lost a lot because of him too. I don't think any of us will be genuinely happy until that evil prick is long dead," Abby said. Al nodded in agreement, looking deep in thought. It seemed like letting Albert know that he wasn't alone helped him a bit. After losing so many people in his life, it was not surprising that he felt personally attacked or targeted.

"My best friend and boss were killed by his men last winter. A lot more happened, but Liz was a big part of my life for a while. She left a hole," Abby said.

"Liz Duffy?" Al asked. Abby's heart dropped a bit when he said Liz's full name.

"Yes. You know her?" Abby asked.

"I went to Duffy's bar all the time when it first opened. She was a lovely lady," Albert said. "When did you stop working there?"

"When it burned down and Liz died," Abby said, remembering that horrible night. Although she wasn't the one who caused any harm to Liz, her anger did burn down the bar. Abby wished she could have controlled herself more in order to leave the building still standing. That corner just didn't look right without Duffy's bar in the lot. Abby remembered how angry she was when it happened. Her rage was so strong that the gang members' bodies were burned beyond recognition; it took them weeks to identify them.

"I guess we've all suffered from that devil," Al said with emotion in his voice. Al got up and placed Hecate in the chair he was sitting in. Hecate turned around a couple times but lay back down again. "I think I'm going to turn in. I hope this hasn't been too upsetting for you guys," Al said even though he was the one who almost broke down a few times. "The tent is in that box. It's quick and easy to put up. The instructions are in the box too," he said, pointing to a big box he had put beside the table they were sitting at before.

"Thank you again," Joe said. He had stayed quiet for a while, doing his best not to upset Al anymore with such direct personal questions.

"Good night," Al said, walking into his trailer.

"Good night," Abby said back to him.

Joe struggled with the tent while Abby and Hecate continued sitting by the fire. Abby went back to the car and got her bag. She grabbed some of the books and tried to find something that would give up where Alexander was. Most of the passages seemed like riddles. It took a lot of focus to even understand a few lines of it. *Okay, am I just tired or stupid?* she thought to herself. Her eyes lost focus.

"Tired. Definitely tired," she said out loud softly. Hecate purred and rolled on her back. "You're not staying out here. There could be coyotes or wolves," she said, looking at Hecate and loving the warmth from the fire.

"Sorry, what was that?" Joe said from a few feet away.

"I was talking to her," Abby said, pointing at the purr monster.

"It's almost up," Joe said.

Abby went back to reading. The storms were almost over them now. Abby felt a bit of rain on the side of her face. She closed the books and grabbed Hecate. Joe had just secured the tent and went back to the car to grab blankets out of the huge bag of items he packed. Abby gathered her stuff up and walked over to the tent. Joe rushed back over and got inside first. Abby waited while he laid out a thick blanket on the bottom of the tent.

"You can come in now," Joe said. Abby looked back at the fire before getting into the tent. A huge gust of wind blew across the empty field and blew the fire right out. Abby got in the tent, and she slipped off the shoes she had borrowed from Joe just inside the tent. Abby set her bag and Hecate down on the blanket. Joe gave Abby a blanket, and he kept one on his side of the tent. Abby leaned down and closed the opening of the tent. Hecate sniffed around, looking for familiar scents. Abby sat down beside Joe. It was a very roomy tent.

"Do you mind if I go to sleep right away?" Joe asked, trying not to be rude.

Abby nodded. "I'm pretty tired too," she said.

They both lay down and closed their eyes. Hecate cuddled into Abby's legs and went to sleep as well.

Abby woke up many times during the night, every little noise outside putting her on alert. The wind was blowing, and she could hear rain hitting outside the tent. The storms were slowly starting. Abby kept thinking that she was hearing someone walking outside the tent, but each time she got up to look outside, there was no one around, and Al's trailer was still dark.

Abby lay down, looking up at the roof of the tent. She used her backpack for a pillow. Joe was completely asleep. He snored lightly but kept fighting and arguing with someone in his sleep. Hecate had gotten annoyed with Abby's restlessness and decided to sleep by her head instead; she slept against the backpack as well. After another hour of just lying there and staring at nothing, Abby got up. She did her best not to disturb Hecate when she pulled the book she was reading before out of her bag.

Abby read through one of the books entirely now that she had gotten a tiny bit of sleep and her eyes were no longer bothering her. She read that the only way to close the gates of hell once they were open was to kill the bridge. The bridge was the person who had opened it in the first place. So basically, the book was telling

Abby what she already knew—that she had to kill Alexander. Everything she came across made her feel like garbage for not killing him when she had the chance. Abby closed the book; she didn't want to keep reading about all the things Alexander could do simply because she let him live last winter. Abby put the book away and lay back down, hoping to get at least one more hour of sleep before having to correct her mistake.

Abby woke up again, this time feeling more refreshed than before. The rain had finally stopped, and it was silent again—for a moment anyway. Abby heard someone moving around outside. This time she was certain of it. She opened the tent a little bit and looked out.

"Good morning!" Al said cheerfully. Abby nodded her head at the cheerful old man.

"Morning," she said back to him. It definitely didn't look like morning; it was darker than night outside.

"Coffee is ready!" Al yelled. Abby was looking around outside but was startled when Joe began to stir behind her. Hecate was still lying on her back against the backpack. Joe only moved around for a moment before getting comfortable again and trying to go back to sleep. Abby shook him a little.

"It's morning," she whispered to her doozy cousin.

"It looks like night still," Joe said, opening one of his eyes and looking out the opening in the tent.

"Yeah, that's why you need to get up. I think we need to find Alexander before today is over," Abby said. Joe sat up and rubbed his eyes.

"I thought we had more time," he said, trying to understand what was happening.

"Let's go talk to Al and then leave," Abby said. She woke up Hecate by picking her up off the bag. Abby repacked her bag and then used the blanket she had used to cover herself during the night to wrap Hecate in since the weather was so unpredictable. Abby took her stuff and left the tent. She went over and sat with Albert. He had three large candles lighting up his small table, and the dim light from his trailer was on. Abby sat down across Albert and pulled out the chair next to her. She set Hecate down on the chair. Hecate moved around and got comfortable without leaving the plush blanket.

"Where's he?" Al asked. Abby shrugged her shoulders and looked over at the tent.

"He's difficult to wake up, it seems," Abby answered. Al smiled and accepted her answer. Abby looked over at the tent after she heard some movement in there.

"I remembered that you only take cream in your coffee," Albert said, handing her a cup that was already made.

"Thank you," Abby said, hoping that was enough.

"I don't remember what your cousin takes in his though," Albert said. Abby laughed.

"That's okay. I have no idea either," she said. Joe finally came out of the tent and walked over to the table they were sitting at. He touched the chair that Hecate was on, and Abby put her hand on it.

"This one is taken," she said, smiling. Joe didn't smile back and just grabbed another foldout chair and sat down.

"He's not a morning person, eh?" Al asked. Abby shook her head no. Albert put a clean mug and the pot of coffee in front of Joe.

He grabbed it and fixed his own coffee. Abby looked over after he was done to see him staring at a watch from his pocket.

"It can't actually be morning. It looks like midnight," Joe said. Abby already drank most of her coffee.

"I'm afraid we'll have to leave in a few minutes," Abby said to Albert.

"The least I can do is make you two something for the road," Albert said. Abby tried to tell him that it wasn't needed, but he wouldn't hear it and hurried inside his trailer. Joe drank most of his coffee and barely spoke. He was definitely not a morning person. He walked back to the tent and grabbed the blankets that he had already folded up. He put them back in the bag in the truck of the car. Albert came back out just as Joe was coming back up the driveway.

"I made you both ham-and-cheese sandwiches. I didn't have much," he said, handing a brown paper bag to Abby.

"I don't know exactly what you two are planning on doing, but I do hope you're both safe," said Albert, hugging Abby and smiling over at Joe. It was clear why Albert couldn't live in Harmon anymore. Someone that kind wouldn't last a minute in that city. Abby said goodbye to Albert and picked up Hecate. Albert reached into the blanket and petted Hecate gently on the head. She barely even moved. Abby walked over to the car where Joe was already standing.

"Would you prefer I drive?" Abby asked since Joe was so tired.

"No, I'll be fine," Joe replied.

Abby got in the passenger side and flung her bag in the back. She put Hecate down between her feet while she buckled up. Joe started the car and turned it around so they wouldn't have to back out of a long, dark driveway.

"So where are we going?" Joe asked. Abby didn't even know now; she just knew that today was the day they needed to find him.

"My place," Abby said. Joe's eyes widened. Now it finally looked like he was waking up.

"Your place?" Joe said, surprised.

"Yeah, we can see if he's there or if he's been there," Abby said. Joe looked uncomfortable.

"And if he shows up while we're there?" Joe asked.

Abby smiled. "We're looking for him. If he delivers himself to us, then that's his problem," Abby said, wishing it would be that easy.

They finally got to the end of the driveway. The main road to town was completely dead. Joe looked around cautiously before creeping out onto the road. The storms were totally surrounding the city of Harmon now—almost like the city was being held hostage by Mother Nature.

Joe got to the edge of town and slowed down even more before entering. His plan was to drive safely and directly to the middle of Harmon in Townsquare, but because there was such a shortage of emergency workers, a lot of things hadn't been cleared off the road yet. Even tow-truck drivers were refusing to go out into the streets of Harmon until Alexander was caught for good, just like last winter. Joe had to back up the car multiple times after learning that some of the roads leading to Townsquare were blocked by vehicles and other debris.

Looking around the city now made Abby realize that Harmon was in even worse condition than it was in the winter. Alexander was closer than ever to accomplishing his evil goals. It had kept Abby up at night thinking about how she had let him live, enabling him to continue his evil existence. It would be so much easier to let her evil urges flow and not care anymore—that had crossed Abby's mind often.

Joe pulled into Townsquare. The bodies had been removed from the streets finally, but the cars were still there. Blood still stained the areas where the innocent had lay dead. Joe drove through Townsquare slowly, making sure to look for hazards. Joe's plan was to park behind the new city hall building, or what was left of it, but it was blocked off by police tape. The yellow tape shined under the light of their headlights that was breaking through the darkness. Joe pulled up as close as he could to the far side of Townsquare and parked.

Abby looked at the pile of rubble and smiled. She had thought about that evil building burning to the ground every day, and it finally happened.

"You look happy for some reason," Joe said, looking over at Abby. She quickly wiped the smile off her face. She was happy that the building was gone, but she knew that she shouldn't be smiling around the burn site. There was a huge loss of life there.

Abby grabbed her bag from the back seat. Hecate looked up at Abby, waiting to see what would happen next. Abby dumped out the books that were clogging her bag and picked up Hecate. She put her back in the bag and secured the zipper. Abby could feel the rumbling from Hecate's purrs while she held the bag.

"So it's just in the tunnels?" Joe asked. Abby got out of the car and put her bag on her back.

"Yeah, just follow me," Abby said. She walked through the police tape past the burnt rubble and to the back of the grounds. From where they were, she decided it would be easier if they were to go through the tunnel at the back of the old building's grounds since the chief had unsealed it anyway. Abby got to the opening with Joe not too far behind her. She pulled on the cover, and it flung open. Joe pulled out a flashlight from his pocket and shined it into the opening. The wind was starting to get worse again, and the darkness from the storms surrounding them still hadn't dissipated.

Abby climbed into the tunnel first while Joe looked on with concern. Abby got to the tunnel and jumped off the metal ladder. There were so many wet footprints going in and out of the tunnels. Since Abby had begun occupying this area, it was only ever hers and Ryan's shoe prints around the tunnels, but now the secret was out. Joe jumped down from the ladder, startling Abby.

"Your place is popular, eh?" Joe said, looking at the shoe prints with Abby.

"It's not supposed to be," Abby said, continuing to walk until she came to the opening for the second level. Abby pulled the huge stone off the top of the opening. Joe ran over to help drag it out of the way. Abby looked down the dark hole. Joe looked at Abby, unaware of where to go next. Abby jumped into the hole and grabbed the ladder. She climbed down to the second tunnel where Alexander used to dwell in the winter. Joe wasn't far behind. He got down to the tunnels too and looked around.

"So this is where he lived," Joe said. It seemed like he was surprised to be there; he wasn't expecting a tour of Alexander's old hideout.

"One more level," Abby said, looking at the metal door on the floor. The metal door was usually covered by an old rug or something, but now it was just closed and kept out in the open. Abby opened the door and climbed down. The door at the bottom of the stairs was open already. She pushed into the door in order to see if anyone was still in her place. Once again, Joe startled her by jumping down too loudly.

After peeking in for a moment, Abby finally walked in. She quickly got upset. Everything in the apartment, every single possession she had, was either broken, torn up, or ruined in some way. Drawers were pulled apart, and clothing was shredded. The bed looked like someone knifed it over and over again. Anything breakable was smashed. Abby stood in the middle of the place she wanted to be her home looking distraught.

"I'm guessing you weren't expecting this?" Joe said. Abby didn't speak; she was starting to feel rage returning like never before. This wasn't her home; the city of Harmon wasn't even her home anymore. She couldn't stop looking around at the mess Alexander or his zombie-like slaves had done. It was such a beautiful and organized apartment before. Abby looked behind her at the door again. Even her hellhounds hadn't returned yet, and Abby had no idea how to actually look for them. Joe walked into the small room to the side that held the bathroom and kitchen.

"Damn!" he yelled. Abby sat down on a ripped-up chair. Joe came rushing out. "It's not much better in there," Joe said. Abby sat quietly while Joe kept looking around. She was thinking about how close she was to finally being home and how fast it all got taken away from her. She was starting to feel the good that was holding her back drain out of her.

15

$\mathscr{A}$bby sat on the floor with boxes around her. She was going through her things since it was unlikely she would ever return there after all this new crap happening. Joe looked around for things that hadn't been destroyed, but there wasn't much. For clothing, Abby was left with a single pair of jeans, her older leather jacket, and a few tank tops. Someone had ripped the heels off her only other pair of boots, but she was able to find glue and was trying to put them back together.

Joe took note of what Abby was doing, and he went to the kitchen and bathroom to collect any food or products of Abby's that hadn't been destroyed. Hecate was still in the bag that was now off of Abby's back and sitting beside her. Abby didn't want her to be out in the apartment in case Alexander came back suddenly. Ryan may have said that Hecate was much more than she appears, but Abby had never seen that side of her. Other than being a tiny bit of a fire starter, Hecate always appeared to be a regular cat to Abby. She only weighed about nine pounds, and she was a little small even for a regular cat. Abby finished up with the last box of items she was going through and then turned and petted Hecate's head, which was poking out of the open backpack.

Joe came back into the open apartment after being in the kitchen and bathroom for a while. He set down two medium-sized bags of items he was able to find.

"Is that it?" Abby asked. Joe looked down at the bags.

"There wasn't much left that they didn't destroy. It was the cops, by the way. I found this," Joe said, tossing a badge on the floor next to Abby. "It was on your kitchen floor next to some smashed plates," he added.

Abby knew that the police were under Alexander's influence and that they were victims too, but she couldn't help but feel some resentment toward them, especially since she warned them not to get too close to Alexander in the first place and they just completely disregarded what she said. Abby didn't think that they deserved what they got, but the officers did invite the evil in after being warned. It was unfortunate, but it was easier for Abby to accept and move on from the deaths of the cops because of how much she warned them and was ignored.

Abby got up from the floor and pointed to a pile of boxes. "I only found a few things," she added. Joe went back into the kitchen and found another bag to put her remaining items in. It appeared Abby was going to be starting over yet again. She was beginning to dislike even being inside the city of Harmon and wanted to move far away from it now more than ever before.

Abby walked around her apartment one last time before leaving it for good. She looked at the mess of her home, now trying to accept that it was never her home to begin with. Joe gathered the bags by the door and waited quietly while Abby took one last look for anything she may be able to salvage. Abby stopped when she got to the bed. It was so messed up that she hadn't noticed the photo that was under one of the shredded blankets. The corner of the picture just happened to catch her eye while she was giving everything a once-over. Abby sat on the bed and pulled the picture out.

"Oh crap," she said as she looked at the picture.

"What?" Joe said, still across the large room by the door. Abby got up and walked over to where Hecate was still on the floor in the backpack. She picked the bag up and put it on her back, then she walked over to Joe in the doorway. She handed him the picture and demanded that they leave immediately.

It was a picture of Abby and Ryan, smiling, looking like the perfect couple. It was taken after the events that happened in the winter and before the current disaster when they were actually able to be happy for a few months. The picture looked normal except Ryan's face was completely scratched out. Joe didn't seem like he was Ryan's biggest fan, but even he felt uneasy after seeing the picture and knew that something was wrong. Joe dropped the picture and grabbed the bags from the apartment as he followed Abby.

Abby climbed as fast as she could up the stairs. She got to the top tunnel and looked at the opening. It was so dark that no light was shining through the tunnel like it usually did. Even at night, the moonlight would shine, but tonight, there wasn't even a moon—just darkness. It was like the stars had sensed what evil was coming and abandoned them. Abby decided to continue going up and get out of the hatch at the back of the Townsquare grounds. She quickly climbed up the small metal stairs and pushed the opening, but it was stuck. Joe found a dry, safe place to set the bags he was carrying and came up the stairs to try and help her. He used the flashlight from his pants' pocket again, making it much easier for both of them to see. Joe tried as hard as he could. He even rammed the hatch with his shoulder, making the whole tunnel rumble a bit, but it wouldn't budge.

"I guess we're going the long way," Abby said, looking down at the opening of the tunnel. Joe put the flashlight in his mouth and picked up the bags again. Just as they started walking toward the tunnel opening, they both stopped and looked at each other. There was the figure of a man doing something at the opening of the tunnel. Abby grabbed her head. A strong evil presence wasn't far from them. Alexander was very close.

"I think it's one of Alexander's," Abby said. Before they could even react, the dark figure ran from the tunnel as fast as he could.

"That's not a good sign," Joe said. Abby smelled something similar to the smells she experienced when the new city hall blew up.

"Shit," Abby said. But before either of them could react, a large explosion sent them flying backward farther into the tunnel. Abby landed on her side. She tried to tug on her backpack to check Hecate, but she had hit her head hard during the fall and could barely move or see. She knew that staying conscious with a head injury was important, but she couldn't fight the pain and the urge to pass out.

Abby woke up a short time later. Her head was still killing her, and her vision was blurred. It took her a moment of opening and closing her eyes to finally get things into focus. She was propped up against the wall of the tunnel, and her backpack was now on her lap. She touched it, and Hecate stirred a bit and blurted out a little meow.

"She's fine," Joe said. He sounded annoyed and out of breath. Abby looked over to where the voice was coming from. Joe had propped his flashlight up on some rocks so he could see while he tried to dig them out. Abby opened her eyes wider and put her bag beside her. The explosion had trapped them in the tunnel; the opening was completely buried.

"You stay there," Joe said, pointing at Abby as she struggled to get up and help.

"I thought you broke your neck. You wouldn't be alive if you were anyone else," Joe said.

"Lucky me," Abby said sarcastically. Joe kept digging. He wiped around and threw another rock into the darkness behind them in the tunnel.

"I don't suppose you know another way out of here?" Joe asked. Abby flinched in pain as she shook her head no.

"Your sword is in the car, right?" Abby asked quietly, trying not to disturb her already aching head.

"Unfortunately. That would have cut through all of this," he said, touching his waistband where he usually put the weapon.

It took Abby a few minutes, but she finally got to her feet. She looked around. With how far inside the tunnel they were buried, she knew they would never be able to dig out. She put her bag back on her back and walked farther into the tunnel and found the metal stairs leading to the opening on the Townsquare grounds. She shook her head for a moment to try to clear her vision again before climbing the stairs. When she got to the top, she looked down the tunnel. She could barely see the light from Joe's flashlight. Abby pushed at the opening and struggled but couldn't get it to budge.

The combination of the frustration she was feeling and the pain in her head was sending her over the edge. As soon as she felt her skin start to heat up, she thought about Alexander and everything else she hated and wanted gone. She placed her hands on the seal and stared at it with her beautifully evil eyes while it creaked and cracked, its structure giving into Abby's force. It didn't take long before the hatch melted and the remaining bit fell around Abby back into the tunnel. A huge rock blocked Abby's way from getting out. Right as she was about to take care of it, Joe came up behind her.

"Wow, good job," he said, clearly happy that he would be able to stop digging. The large rock was shaking on unsteady ground now that the hatch to the opening was gone. Joe went into a small run with the little room he had and hit the rock with his shoulder. It fell over on the other side, giving them room to finally get out of the tunnels. Abby got up onto solid ground and put her hands on her knees and leaned over. She may heal faster than regular people, but she wasn't given any time to do that.

Joe climbed back down into the tunnel and came back up right away with the bags of items he repacked after the explosion. Joe looked around for a moment, disorientated.

"That way?" he asked, pointing to a small amount of light poking through the heavy darkness in Townsquare.

"Yeah, and thanks," Abby said, referring to him picking her up after the explosion.

"Don't mention it. I wouldn't be a very good cousin if I left you lying there," he said, trying to lighten up the situation, but Abby didn't respond. Normally she was the one trying to break through something serious with sarcasm, but now wasn't the time. Joe picked up the bags again and tried to walk close to Abby. He made his concern over her head injury obvious, but Abby was already starting to feel better. Getting out of the tunnel into normal air helped a lot. She just needed time to deal with everything that was happening, but it seemed like time was never on her side.

"I hope we're not too late," Joe said. Abby looked at him, confused. "For Ryan?" he said.

Abby gasped. She had almost forgotten where they were going before the explosion happened.

"How long were we under there for?" she asked as she hustled faster to the car.

"Approximately an hour," Joe said. Abby got to the car and waited for Joe to unlock it; he was putting the bags in the trunk first. Even though Abby knew that she couldn't continue spending time with Ryan, it didn't change her feelings for him or her concern over his well-being.

Abby got in the car and looked in the mirror. The bleeding from her head seemed to have stopped, but the cut was still visible and tender to the touch. Abby had her bag by her feet, and she pulled it up on her lap. Hecate poked her face out of the bag and looked up at Abby. Her face was so expressive; it looked like she knew how Abby felt and what was going through her very busy mind.

Joe got in the driver's side of the car after getting his sword out of the trunk and putting it in the back seat. "Me driving was a good call," Joe said as he looked at the deep cut that was slowly healing on Abby's head.

"I could have driven if you wanted," Abby said even though she was unsure of the point she was trying to argue.

"Absolutely. You could drive right now, just not well," Joe said. Abby couldn't argue with that. Her vision was finally clear, but the blinding pain kept coming and going. She placed her head in her hands. Hecate purred around her head now that it was closer to her lap.

"I guess it's a good thing we're heading to the hospital," Joe said. Abby looked up. They were already driving. She didn't even hear him start the car.

"I'm not going to the hospital for me," Abby said, being difficult like always.

"I'd tell them to restrain you for treatment if I didn't think you would melt the restraints," Joe said, trying to joke. Abby smiled a bit, giving him enough of a reaction to continue trying to joke the whole way there. Abby tried carrying a conversation, but Joe's voice kept sounding like it was fading. In fact, everything was fading again.

16

*A*bby opened her eyes. She was lying in a hospital bed. The pain in her head was completely gone now. She looked around as her eyes focused. She wasn't in a hospital room, but she was in the hallway on a stretcher, along with many other people. Nurses were running up and down the hallways, frantically trying to care for the overabundant patients. Abby sat up, and a nurse came over to her.

"Ma'am, I need you to lie back down," the nurse said. "You have a head injury." The nurse reached for the bandage on Abby's head. Abby put her hand up and blocked the nurse's hand.

"There was a guy with me. Where is he?" Abby asked bluntly.

"You have a visitor in the lounge. I'll go get him," the nurse said. Abby watched her walked away. Once she was gone, Abby ripped the IV line out of her arm. Luckily, most of the people around her in the hospital hallway were all unconscious anyway and didn't have to see that. Abby grabbed her clothes, which were hanging on the bottom of the stretcher she was on. She looked for the bag with Hecate in it but didn't see it.

"She's probably with Joe," Abby said to herself, trying not to lose her cool yet. She had a feeling that all her evil abilities were going to be needed soon anyway. Keeping her cool all the time meant that her outburst would be much more powerful.

Abby rushed to a bathroom at the end of the hall she was in. She quickly changed out of the stupid hospital gown. *Why?* Abby asked herself. She never understood hospital gowns. *Just make them so they can close somehow, such a ridiculous design.*

Once Abby got dressed, she looked in the mirror over the small sink. She pulled her hair back off her face and peeled the bandage off her head. It was completely healed, not even a scar. That's a huge reason why she never liked being admitted to hospitals. If a doctor saw that, they would probably dissect her.

Abby got herself together and put her jacket on. She peeked out the bathroom. Joe and the nurse were walking away from her empty stretcher. Abby slipped out of the bathroom and went through a door next to it that led to an elevator. As she stood there waiting for the elevator, she felt something odd. It wasn't just an uneasy feeling; it was multiple feelings at the same time. It gave her stomach butterflies. She looked around. The uneasy feeling got much worse as she walked toward the door leading to the stairs. She looked through a tiny square window in the top-left corner of the door.

Three men dressed all in black were starting to climb the stairs; their eyes looked dark and tired, like the rest of Alexander's mind-controlled victims. But unlike Alexander's other victims, these men were huge and built like bodybuilders. They were carrying briefcases, and Abby saw a gun on one of their belts.

"Ryan," Abby said quietly. Abby looked at the men until they were out of sight on the second floor. The sound of the elevator arriving startled Abby out of her thoughts. She looked back as a bunch of people got out of the elevator and were replaced by a new load. Abby watched the elevator leave. She looked back at the stairs and pushed the door open. She began following the men up the stairs. Abby was light on her feet and so quiet. She stayed far enough behind them that they didn't see her but close enough that she could hear which door they went through.

They stopped at the fourth floor, the floor Abby knew Ryan's room was on. She weighed it in her head. They could have moved Ryan to another room or floor, but their intent wasn't up for debate. Abby can sense evil thoughts, and that's all these guys were having right now. She got closer but stopped when she heard another voice. The men didn't chat among themselves as they walked up the stairs; clearly under Alexander's trance, they only had their assignment on their minds. This voice identified himself as security. He requested to see ID. Abby couldn't see what was going on, but she heard him demand a response a few times. One of the men finally said three words: "Let us pass."

The security guard once again requested ID and a reason for their visit. Abby heard the guard grunt a little, and then the heavy door to the fourth floor opened and closed. She slowly moved up the stairs to the fourth floor. A man in a security uniform was lying just outside the door. Abby got closer. The scene was horrific. His throat was cut, and he was grabbing at it and gasping for air as he bled out. Abby pulled an emergency cord that was hanging from the sealing just outside the door.

She rushed inside the door so anyone who came to help the guard wouldn't see her. Before she got in the door, she noticed a small security camera pointing at where the assault took place. For a moment, she was worried that people would come looking for her; she didn't like having to fight off innocent people who were only following orders or doing their job. But then she realized that they would be more focused on finding the three people who killed him instead of trying to find some girl who made them aware of the emergency. Lately, Abby had been rationalizing things to herself a lot.

Abby saw the men enter a room in the distance. She rushed to him but was stopped by a nurse.

"Can I help you?" the nurse asked. Abby looked past her at the room she was trying to get to.

"No, thanks," she said, dismissing her.

"Ma'am, I need you to at least sign in as a visitor," the nurse said, standing in front of Abby. Abby heard a male's scream coming from the room the men went into. The nurse turned a bit when she heard it.

"I have to go," Abby said, trying to move the nurse's arm that was barring her, but the bitch wouldn't budge. Abby knew she was just doing her job, but she punched her right in the face and knocked the fat bitch on her ass. Other nurses ran to their colleague. They gave Abby the stink eye, but she didn't care. She was now Abby to run past them.

She got to the room just as a gun went off. Now the nurses who were cradling their asshole coworker were freaking out and running toward the stairs to evacuate the floor; they even left their patients behind. By the look of them, they would probably trample the bleeding security guard to save their own asses. Abby walked into the room. One of the men was on the floor and looked to be dead.

"Abby?" Ryan said, a gun still in his shaking hand. Chief Doyle was Ryan's roommate, but he was still in a forced coma due to the burns all over his body. The two other men were standing near the bottom of Ryan's bed, not even acknowledging that one of them was dead.

"Finish it," Abby said. Ryan looked at the men and back to Abby. He wasn't a killer, and the only time he was ever violent was when he spent too much time around Abby. Ryan squinted and fired two more rounds, hitting the men. They both fell to the ground, blood pouring out of them.

"They're going to keep coming, aren't they?" Ryan asked even though he already knew the answer.

"They'll probably keep coming for both of you," Abby said, looking at the chief as well. It seemed like Alexander didn't like people surviving after he controlled their minds.

"I don't think he can be moved yet," Ryan said. Abby looked at Ryan as he got out of bed. He was back to the same old Ryan who had moved across the hall from her half a year ago. It made her feel terrible that she couldn't spend time with him without turning him into something he's not.

Abby stayed with Ryan for a few minutes, trying to think of a way to keep both him and Chief Doyle safe from Alexander. Abby thought about her hellhounds and tried reaching out to them in thought. It always felt like their minds were connected. It had been so long since she saw them. They had evacuated the tunnels when she told them to and stayed hidden so well. Abby closed her eyes and tried envisioning where they were so she could get them. She heard people screaming and saw Joe demanding that people get out of the way. She opened her eyes.

"They're here already," Abby said, surprised.

"Oh no. You remember how much damage and killing they did the last time they were in this hospital, don't you?" Ryan said. Abby gave him a weird look.

"They killed Alexander's men before his men could kill anyone else. Call me heartless if you want, but I don't see that as a big loss," Abby said. She was unprepared to defend the hounds, especially to Ryan. He had seen them in action and had been saved by them before. Abby wasn't impressed with his attitude toward the hounds now.

Ryan sat on the edge of the bed, and Abby stood by the bottom of it beside the bodies. The door to the room burst open. Abby was expecting it to be security because of the gunshots, but it was Joe who stepped inside.

"I've been looking everywhere for you," he said. Joe looked at Ryan who was pointing his gun at Joe. He was startled by the rough way he entered the room. "Wow, there's also a security dead in the stairway. They just took him away," Joe said, looking at the three dead bodies lying in a pool of blood.

"Damn," Abby said. She was hoping her small effort to alert someone to the guard's emergency would save him, but the cut on his throat was really deep.

Before Abby could get Ryan and Joe up to speed together, screams of terror filled the hallway as the remaining people on the floor scattered. Joe closed the door and leaned in to lock it.

"It's okay," Abby said. Joe looked confused. Abby had forgotten that Joe had only read about hellhounds; he hadn't been around when they were present, until now. Joe cracked the door open to look out, and as he peeked through the crack, his eyes met a hound's. He stared into the shiny red eyes of the evil beast before backing up. The hounds used their large bodies to force open the door and enter the room. Joe looked like he was amazed but very unprepared to meet them right now.

They growled at him as they passed by, displaying their hate for his father without attacking. Abby walked up to the hounds and threw her arms around one of their necks. "I didn't realize how much I missed you guys," Abby said, finally feeling whole again now that her beasts were back. Abby paused for a moment, remembering her special beast.

"Where's Hecate?" she asked, turning to Joe.

"In the car," Joe said, trying not to draw the attention of the hellhounds since he wasn't too sure about his safety with them yet. Abby whispered to her hounds before rising to her feet again.

"It's probably best for you to stay here with the chief," Abby said, looking at Ryan. Ryan nodded, giving Joe a weird look.

"What about the bodies?" Joe asked, looking at them with disgust.

"The hounds will eat them," Abby said bluntly. Joe walked wide-eyed to the door.

"So I get to stay here guarded by giant dogs that are eating people?" Ryan asked.

Abby turned before she got to the door and looked at Ryan. "No. You get to live once again because of the hounds, and they'll only eat the dead people unless he sends more for them to kill," Abby said, unsure of Ryan's attitude. He had always displayed distrust for the hellhounds. At first, Abby completely understood it. He was only human, and seeing those beasts for the first time could change the way you look at the world. But they had proven themselves in front of him multiple times; the distrust should have faded.

Ryan lay back down on his bed without even saying goodbye to Abby. A couple more hounds entered as she and Joe slipped out the door. There were around ten in the small room now, so the bodies wouldn't last long.

The floor was basically abandoned, and the scared nurses were gone. Even if they were in real danger from the hounds, there was no one left to help them. Almost all the Harmon police officers were dead, and the security for the hospital was probably dealing with everything, including the death of one of their own.

Abby and Joe walked to the stairs. The body of the security guard was gone, but his blood hadn't been cleaned up. The nurses likely didn't have time before they started running from the hounds. Abby walked around the blood and started going down the stairs.

"So Ryan seems nice," Joe said sarcastically.

"He's been through a lot," Abby said in a pathetic attempt to normalize his behavior.

"The hounds, though. They're huge. I felt like they wanted to kill me," Joe said.

"They did," Abby said bluntly.

"But I didn't threaten them or you," Joe said, trying to understand.

"They're hellhounds. Their first instinct is to kill and mutilate," Abby explained. Joe wanted to continue chatting as they descended on the stairs, but he got lost inside his own head. He had only seen Abby use her abilities when she had to, and this was the first time he saw the hellhounds. Abby looked at him as she got close to the bottom level. It was obvious that he was in a bit of a shock. Joe may have more insight into who Abby was more than anyone else, but it seemed like he never believed she was actually meant to be evil like the hounds, until now.

"If you no longer want to be a part of this, I understand," Abby said, hoping to calm his fears.

"No, it's fine. I knew who you were and who your father is. I've seen you walk through fire like it was nothing. I don't know why this threw me off so much," he explained.

Abby nodded. She knew why. It was because anyone who wasn't programmed to be evil wasn't meant to be around hellhounds; they were meant to be killed by them.

Abby and Joe reached the bottom floor. They quickly rushed toward the exit of the hospital. Abby walked past the nurse she had ran from originally. She put her coat up to hide her face so she wouldn't have to knock out another nurse. Abby and Joe went outside, and she followed him to where he parked the car. Hecate was awake for once and looking out at them like she was waiting for them to come back.

Abby got in the passenger seat again, and Joe got in the driver's side. Hecate jumped into the front seat and sat on Abby's lap. The streets were even darker now, and the street lights have all been smashed again. Abby looked around. Tt was obvious that tonight was the night Alexander was going to try and send the world into the darkness he craved.

Abby reached into the back of the car and opened the book she was reading at Al's trailer—the pages Alexander left open on Joe's table. Abby finally showed the passage to Joe. "This was one of the pages he left open on your table, and the page he was focused on," she said. Joe flipped the bag. There was one missing. Only a small number of paper remained on the book's seam from where it was ripped out.

"So you think he plans on opening the gates of hell?" Joe asked. Abby nodded.

"And I think he ripped out the pages with the directions on how to stop it. There's only one way listed, but in order to do that, we have to let it happen first," Abby said.

Joe and Abby looked at each other. Tt didn't have to be said how risky that was, but if they killed Alexander right after he became the bridge between hell and earth, then they would be rid of him forever. Joe put the car into drive.

"Where are you going?" Abby asked him. They didn't even know where he would be opening the bridge yet.

"My place. I have to make sure I have all my weapons if we're actually battling Alexander while hell is rising," Joe said the words but still couldn't believe they were coming out of his mouth. Abby could tell this was a little overwhelming for Joe. He had been on the run from his bloodline his whole life, and now he was standing and fighting against it. Both Joe and Abby were hardened to killing because of having to do so to simply survive, but this was different. Either they succeed or everyone dies—not just in the city of Harmon, but everywhere.

17

*T*he streets were bare except for a few cars trying to leave now that the darkness was completely over Harmon. All the surrounding darkness that caused nearby towns to be evacuated to Harmon was now right over them.

"Why would he gather everyone here?" Joe said. It sounded like he was thinking out loud. "Is some kind of large sacrifice needed?"

"I think he wanted to fully stock a food source for what he's releasing," Abby said. She looked out the window at the darkness. She looked to the side of the road, but she could barely even see the sidewalk. It was so dark. Joe's eyes were focused on the road. He was only able to see as far as the headlights lit up in front of them.

Way off in the distance, flames broke through the darkness. It looked like a large dark-colored pickup truck with a cap similar to the one they borrowed from Rory and his partner to take the chief to the hospital. They got closer, and Abby noticed that it was in fact the exact same truck. Joe pulled to the side of the road after noticing it was the truck belonging to the firefighters.

Abby picked up Hecate and gently placed her on the back seat. She got out and slammed the door, not even noticing Joe right behind her. Joe stood back, unable to stand the flames. Abby walked up to the car and looked through the smashed windows as she stood in the flames unaffected by them. It was Rory and his partner. They were still in uniform but very dead.

"Well?" Joe asked as he held his hands up, blocking the bright flames from his eyes. Abby took a moment before answering and looked at Rory, thinking about the random but special moment they shared together. She finally broke herself away from the sight of another person she liked killed.

"Was it the fire?" Joe asked.

Abby shook her head. "They both had bullets in their head," Abby said. She wanted to cry and get upset, but instead of sadness taking control of her, it was anger.

"Should we stop the fire and bury the bodies?" Joe asked, trying to be respectful since he knew that Abby had been with Rory.

"They're dead. If fire's good enough for the Vikings, it's good enough for them. Just drive," Abby said. Although she was trying to act cold about the deaths, it was obvious on her face that they affected her. After losing Liz, she was hoping that the only people dying around her from now on would be Alexander's men, but that was just wishful thinking. During war, deaths from both sides should be expected. And that's exactly what Alexander wanted—to rage war on the living.

Hecate climbed back on Abby's lap as Joe slowly drove them away from the sad scene. Hecate put her small paws up on the window, and she and Abby looked out of it at the fire. Abby closed her eyes, hoping she would open them again and be back in her place, living in peace. But she realized a while ago that normal lives were for normal people, and unfortunately, she was so far from normal that she looked insane in the rearview mirror.

Abby pulled the book from the back seat again and tried to understand more of it.

"I read that the bridge opens at the point where Alexander draws most of his power, but wasn't that the new city hall building that was destroyed?" Joe asked.

"The building wouldn't be needed, just the grounds, if that's it." Abby replied.

"Could it be the hospital since that's where he gathered all those people?" Joe asked.

Abby thought for a moment. "I don't think so," she said, although she wasn't completely sure. It wouldn't make sense for him to gather everyone there just to kill them without purpose. Also, Alexander never spent much time at the hospital, so that location wouldn't work. Everything pointed to him using Townsquare as the site.

Joe pulled into his lot quickly. Abby put Hecate in the back of the car so she could wait there. They quickly walked into the darkened building. Normally the hall lights stayed on twenty-four hours, but they were out tonight, matching the darkness the rest of the town was in. His door was smashed in again. Alexander clearly had people out looking for him too. Joe rushed to grab a few things. He put a small handgun on his belt. It seemed like that was the main thing he came back for. Abby looked out the window behind his couch; it was still dark. She couldn't make out anything. Joe squeezed past her and sat down on the end of the couch. He picked up his bong, which was still sitting on the floor beside him, and put a small bit of weed in it.

"Seriously?" Abby said, wondering why he would think this was the right time for something like that.

"I saw hellhounds today. This is happening," Joe said bluntly before taking a huge puff and coughing for a few minutes. He got up after he was done and grabbed some food from his cupboard. "Do you want anything?" he asked. Abby didn't answer. She walked out the apartment into the dark hallway to head back to the car. As she got to the end of the hall, she could hear Joe struggling to close his damaged door behind him.

Abby went outside and waited near the car. Joe came out of the building, running after Abby. He unlocked the car and got in first. The smell of weed followed him. Abby opened her door and went to get in, but a hand from the darkness grabbed her wrist and threw her on the ground outside the car. A black hooded figure holding a knife stood over Abby. Hecate jumped on the passenger seat and looked down at Abby with her shining yellow eyes, then began to change color; a hint of red was added to her eyes.

The figure got closer to the car and bent down, still clinging to his knife. Abby put her hand on the passenger seat to help herself get up. Before either Joe or the hooded figure could use their blades, Hecate reached over Abby with her paw and swatted the hooded figure, scratching him across the face. He fell to the ground near Abby as she hurried to her feet.

Joe got out of the car and ran over. He turned on his flashlight and looked at the guy who was grabbing at his face in pain now. The cut looked like it was minor at first, but somehow it burned and sizzled like acid was eating away at his skin. Joe looked at

Hecate, who was now sitting in the seat looking completely innocent.

"I thought Ryan was crazy when he said she attacked Alexander at his place," Joe said, looking at the tiny black cat. Abby was finally standing again, and the guy on the ground had stopped moving. Steam continued coming from his face, but instead of looking, Abby just got in the car and set Hecate on her lap again.

Joe slowly walked around to the driver's side. He kept looking back at what was probably a dead body now. He got in the driver's side not expecting Hecate to be on Abby's lap again.

"Aren't you worried she'll do something to you?" Joe asked. Both Abby and Hecate looked at him.

"She's had many opportunities to kill me if that's something she wanted to do," Abby said.

Abby and Joe drove to Townsquare. Neither one of them wanted to go there after the killings and explosions, but there wasn't anyone else anymore. The closer they got to Townsquare, the darker it got. They both felt very uneasy, but to Abby, that was a good thing. It meant that they were finally headed in the right direction.

The farther they went into Harmon, the more they saw cars and people trying to get out of the city's center. It seemed like they were the only fools trying to get in. The ten-minute drive more than doubled in time because of having to drive around smashed up cars and debris. Joe tried all the streets leading to Townsquare, but they were all blocked by abandoned vehicles. Finally, he gave up. He parked on the side of the road and started grabbing his gear. Abby put Hecate in her bag again and put it on her back once she got out of the car.

They walked to the edge of Townsquare and looked around. It was too dark to be able to see Alexander from where they were, but Abby noticed something odd. The darkness in the sky directly above Townsquare was moving in a swirling motion. Abby hit Joe's arm and pointed.

"That's not good," Joe said, looking up at the crazy sight.

"It's great actually. It means we're in the right place," Abby said.

"Only my sister could think something like that is great," said a familiar, eerie voice.

"Come out from the shadows, coward," Joe demanded as he drew his sword. Abby looked at Joe acting foolish. What he had already witnessed from Alexander was nothing compared to what he was capable of. But that made her question why Alexander was waiting.

"So if you've gotten all your abilities back, why not just kill us? You know we'll stop you," Abby said as Alexander's slow approach finally stopped. He stood a few feet in front of them, still smiling.

"Why would I want to kill you, my dear sister? I still think we can rule together," Alexander said. Abby rolled her eyes and smirked.

"Rule? I think you mean destroy," Abby said sarcastically, making her brother's creepy smile even wider.

"He just wants an audience," said Joe roughly. The only time Alexander's condescending smile left his face was when he looked at Joe again.

"If you're my audience, I guess you're just in time for the show," Alexander said, turning away from them both. He started to slowly walk back to the pit where the new city hall was. The yellow caution tape was flying off in the wind from the mysterious weather overhead. Joe ran toward Alexander, preparing to assault him from behind—a desperate move. Joe was brought to a halt when the ground beneath them began to shake violently. Abby fell around the same time as Joe, so they lost sight of each other. The only person Abby could see was Alexander. He didn't seem fazed by the ground's angry shakes.

Abby didn't notice Hecate climbing out of her bag during the commotion. The ground split and opened up under Abby's feet. She grabbed onto the side of the opening in the ground as the cement crumbled away. Joe got back on his feet and ran over to help. He reached out and clenched Abby's wrist as soon as she lost her grip and was beginning to fall. Joe pulled Abby away from the open ground since it was growing wider as more of the earth fell into it.

The split led right to where Alexander was now standing on the other side of the pit where the explosion happened. The number of cops and civilians who were killed during that explosion were nothing compared to the death toll Alexander wanted.

"We're too late, aren't we?" Joe asked, looking at the sky swirling over the open earth.

18

Abby tried walking over to Alexander. The wind was so extreme that it was making her fall over. The ground was still moving and was uneven under her feet. Joe was right behind her. He was trying to dodge flying debris from the crazy winds. The swirling clouds looked like they were getting lower over the explosion site. The splits in the ground all met at Alexander's feet, creating a large opening in the earth.

The closer Abby got, the more uneasy she felt. Her head was filled with the most amount of evil she had ever felt. This was even worse than Alexander at his most powerful. Abby got to the edge of the opening and dropped to her knees. She looked across the pit at Alexander. He was looking down into the pit with his arms out like he was welcoming something.

"Did he do it? This is the gates of hell opening, isn't it?" Joe asked. Abby looked into the pit. It was so dark, but the evil sound of something large climbing to the surface was echoing to the top of the opening.

"What's coming?" Joe asked. Abby had a concerned look of shock on her face that Joe hadn't seen before.

"What isn't coming? Anything evil that you can imagine is on its way," Abby said with little breath. She sat down and looked at Joe.

"So this is it? The end?" Joe said, looking around. It definitely looked like the end of the world. Abby tugged at her bag, noticing how much lighter it was.

"Hecate?" Abby yelled, realizing she was gone.

"She probably got herself out of here," Joe said, touching Abby's arm.

"You don't know that!" Abby yelled, pulling away. A huge sign from a business flew through the winds and hit Abby and Joe, and they fell in different directions. Rain poured on Abby as she tried getting up. She stayed on her knees and looked around. Thunder rumbled through the city of Harmon. The only light in the city that night were from the flashes of lightning.

Abby fell back onto the pavement and looked around. She couldn't believe she had failed again. Evil always wins. The lightning flashed once again, revealing the image of Joe running full speed toward Alexander. He jumped over the pit with his sword drawn. Right as his blade was about to make contact with Alexander, he froze. Alexander slowly turned his head to look at Joe, his eyes glowing red and his skin shimmering.

Alexander reached out his hand and grabbed Joe by the neck. Abby watched in terror; she had never felt so helpless. As Alexander's grip on Joe's neck tightened, Joe's body fell limp.

Alexander looked past Joe right into Abby's eyes as he slowly released his grip. Joe's lifeless body fell into the opening at Alexander's feet. Abby couldn't believe what she saw.

"Come," Alexander shouted in a commanding voice in her direction. Abby got up and looked around. There was no sign of Hecate, Ryan was still in the hospital, and she was still processing what had just happened to Joe. She was on her own again. Abby walked toward Alexander. Now she had nothing and no one. She knew that she was supposed to fight against what Alexander was doing, but now she had nothing to fight for. Abby stopped when she got close enough to Alexander to see his face.

"Can't you see it now?" he asked, looking at his sister. Abby looked at him and then around at the mess.

"See what?" she said hopelessly.

"This was always how it was supposed to be. You just have to accept it. We'll be unstoppable," he said. The rumbling and unnerving growls coming from the open earth got louder.

"They're almost here," Alexander said.

Abby had no idea what to expect. She looked on, wondering. There were pictures and ideas of what the underworld held, but there had never been real accounts.

The opening in the ground glowed an eerie reddish orange. The feeling of evil was overwhelming for Abby. She looked away and put her hands up to her head.

"Watch!" Alexander shouted at her. Joe was right; Alexander definitely wanted an audience. Abby tried to deal with the pain in her head from the overwhelming evil that was approaching.

A hand reached up and grabbed the side of the earth near Abby's foot. She moved back as it pulled itself up. It was almost shaped like a human but much larger. There were no features on its face, just an opening for the mouth and indentations for eyes. It looked like magma or walking lava. It even steamed.

Abby watched as more of these lava creatures climbed out of the earth. Were they always down there? Did Alexander just create them? So many questions ran through Abby's head.

"What do you think?" Alexander asked. Abby looked at him and then back at the creatures. As the growling creatures climbed out of the pit, they all stood facing Alexander like they were waiting for orders. Abby stared at them before she was startled out of her thoughts. "Answer me!" Alexander demanded. Abby wasn't even sure what to say.

"What are they?" she asked, stumbling over her words.

"My army," Alexander said with glee. "They aren't much to look at now, but they'll take proper form once they start eating." Abby didn't have to ask what he meant. It also explained why he had begun eating people to gain more power as well.

"So that's why you gathered everyone from all the surrounding towns at the hospital?" Abby asked even though she already knew the answer. Alexander laughed.

"I have to give you credit. You're a smart girl. It must run in the family," he said, laughing.

Alexander waited while the rest of his army climbed to the top. Abby had no idea how many there were now—fifty or a hundred. They all stood around Alexander. The ones that were closer to Abby didn't bother her. They could sense the evil within her and figured she was one of them. Abby reached out and touched one of the lava creatures, and since they had no form, her hand slipped through the hot lava without the creature noticing. Alexander looked at Abby and then back at his army.

"Go. Be strong and feast," Alexander ordered. The creatures growled and began heading in the same direction, toward the hospital.

"No, wait!" Abby yelled, trying to get the attention of the creatures, but they ignored her. The only person who could command them was the person who opened the gate.

"Alexander, please!" she begged, but he ignored her pleas. "Kill me. Take back all the power you want. Just stop this!" He finally turned around and faced his sister.

"You don't get it yet, do you? This is all there is and all there ever was. This is what we're made for. You ripped it apart, but we're still pieces of the same cloth," Alexander said in a crazy, possessed voice.

"Now send the rest," he said, looking back down at the hole.

Abby ran to Alexander, but he threw her to the ground. Abby screamed in frustration. Her frustration turned into anger, causing a small explosion to radiate from where she hit the ground. Alexander fell to the ground as well. He got up quickly and walked over to Abby, but before he could act, Abby heard growling that she was familiar with—her hounds had heard their master's yells.

Their glowing eyes were the only things visible in the darkness as they surrounded the entire exterior of Townsquare. Abby looked around at all the eyes staring at them. She wasn't alone, and she never will be. Alexander was still shocked at the sight. Abby kicked him while he was distracted and ran toward the eyes of her loyal hounds. The hounds at the other end of Townsquare were slowly pushing the lava creatures back into the opening. They were containing the creatures by themselves.

"I wanted to do this together, but you're not going to ruin this again," Alexander yelled as he chased after Abby.

"Go," Abby said, pointing her hounds in the direction of all the creatures. They surrounded the creatures and the pit. More of the creatures tried to climb up, but the hounds ripped them apart and threw them back down. The lava creatures must have known what hellhounds were because none of them willingly challenged the hounds.

Abby ducked into a dark alley that led away from Townsquare. She looked on at her hounds taking care of the situation. Her national anger was what made her abilities stronger. But at the moment, her mind was clouded with worry, failure, and mourning for Joe.

Abby was watching her hounds in action when someone from behind her threw her forcefully into the brick wall at the end of the alley. She lay there for a second as steps walked closer to her. It was Alexander again, clearly pissed off that she was able to mess up his plans for a second time.

"I really don't understand you," he said as he knelt down beside her.

"Likewise," Abby said, pulling herself up.

Alexander smirked. "I guess we're not as alike as I thought," Alexander grabbed Abby's long red hair and wrapped it around his hand. He dragged her out of the alley while she grabbed at his hands. He picked her up by her hair and then grabbed her arm once they got by one of the cracks caused by the cement opening. Alexander held her over the crack in the earth by her arm.

The hellhounds continued getting rid of the lava creatures down the pit. A few of them looked over at Alexander and growled, but they were too late. Alexander dropped Abby into the earth.

As Abby fell, she closed her eyes, accepting what was happening. But something else grabbed her by the shoulder. She opened her eyes, but she could only see black fur. It wasn't the same rough black fur on her loyal hellhounds though.

Abby was roughly tossed on the ground by the huge animal. She didn't notice the pressure its teeth caused to the skin on her shoulder until it released her. It was bigger than the hellhounds. In fact, the hounds that were approaching to attack Alexander were now backing away and focusing back on the lava creatures that were almost gone now.

"What?" Alexander said as it charged toward him. Its growl was more feline than hound. It grabbed Alexander and tossed his body around like a rag doll. When the animal tossed him into the distance toward the hellhounds, Abby was finally able to see its face. It looked like a giant black panther with glowing evil red eyes. Abby looked into its eyes and knew right away.

"Hecate?" Abby said in surprise. Hecate approached Abby and let her touch her head. Abby smiled. She had known that Hecate was so much more than a cat, but she had no idea just how much more.

Alexander yelled as the last one of his lava creatures was sent back down the hole they came from. He looked over at Abby with an angrier look on his face now.

"You think you've stopped me? You've only made this worse!" he shouted. Alexander's eyes glowed as fire swept over Townsquare. It didn't affect Abby or her beasts, but the businesses in the square went up in flames. "I'll burn everything on this earth to the ground!" he shouted like a child having a tantrum. Abby got up and ran to Alexander. She tackled him to the ground, and they fell by the large pit that the creatures climbed out of.

They rolled around, both of them fighting fire with fire and getting nowhere. All they did was cause more damage to the city.

"You should know by now that there's no way to stop either of us," Alexander said with a grin. Abby looked into the pit and back at Alexander.

"Then why don't I send us both back to where we came from?" she said, looking deep into Alexander's widening eyes. Just as she went to push him and allow herself to fall as well, Hecate's large teeth grabbed the bottom of Abby's pants, pulling her back from the pit and making her fall on the ground. She looked up at Hecate standing over her. Alexander got up but was attacked in all directions by huge hellhounds. He tried to fight back, but nothing on earth was a match for the evil beasts.

As Alexander yelled commands to try and take control, the earth began to slowly close. "Nooo!" he screamed over and over again. He struggled to get away from the opening, but the hounds grabbed him. The flesh from his arms tore as the dogs dragged him down to hell.

Abby got up and walked over to the ground. It was completely closed, but she could still hear Alexander's screams as the hellhounds escorted him. Abby looked around at Townsquare. It was completely destroyed, and some of the businesses were still burning. Abby still couldn't believe that Joe was gone. She had just gotten to know him, and he already started feeling like a constant presence in her life. Abby jumped when she felt something on her leg. Hecate was back to her usual size and was purring around Abby.

"You're just full of surprises, aren't you?" Abby said before picking her up.

CHAPTER 19

*A*s Abby picked up her bag and a few things she noticed she dropped, she heard the sound of sirens coming from the distance. Normally this would require a huge amount of emergency response, but there was barely any left. Abby grabbed her stuff and Hecate and got out of Townsquare. Luckily, Ryan's car wasn't in Alexander's damage path. She rushed to the car and got in the driver's side. Joe had left the keys on the driver's seat without Abby noticing, like he knew there was a chance he wasn't going to make it back.

Abby sat in the car for a moment. She wanted to cry and completely break down. Hecate stayed on her lap while she decided what to do. "We should check the hospital," Abby said to herself, thinking about what Joe would suggest they do. Abby started the car and drove to the hospital. Harmon looked like it was in the middle of a brutal war. Abby tried not to focus on anything other than getting to the hospital.

Once she arrived, she saw that the hospital was still standing and everything was fine. Ryan was outside. It looked like he was giving orders to the few cops who were left. Abby wanted to go to him so badly, but she knew that she couldn't. She couldn't be around anyone anymore. That part of her life was over now.

Abby drove away and went to Ryan's apartment building. She dropped off his car and left the keys under the seat. Abby went into the building and stopped at Joe's place. She packed a few food items in her bag and grabbed a picture of Joe off his fridge. She looked at it for a moment before putting it in a zippered side pocket of her bag. Abby put Hecate back in her bag too.

There was nowhere on earth for them since it seemed like they weren't meant to be there anyway. Abby left the building with Hecate and walked to a bus stop. People from the surrounding towns were taking certain buses to get back home. Abby hopped on one of the buses that was going two towns over. She wasn't sure where she would be going from there, but she knew she needed to get as far away from Harmon as possible.

During the bus ride, she couldn't help but overhear many people talking about the events in Harmon. There were different theories that people had come up with. The most common was that it was a government experiment gone wrong. Their voices faded as Abby looked out the window, holding Hecate on her lap. She wondered if she would see her hounds again, and her remaining thoughts drifted between Joe and Ryan. She hadn't even had time to process Rory's death, let alone Joe's.

Abby made a vow to herself right then to never get close to another human being. It was only her and her beasts, no one else. All relationships did was complicate things. Abby closed her eyes, hoping she would stop seeing the events of the day and instead sleep. Hecate curled up on her lap, not caring about where they were going, just happy to be traveling with Abby.

Abby opened her eyes as someone touched her shoulder. "Last stop," said an older man. It was the bus driver. She had fallen asleep after forcing herself to stay awake for so long. Abby grabbed her stuff and picked Hecate up. She got off the bus and looked around. The bus stop was in the middle of nowhere. It was fields for miles around.

"Is this where you wanted to be?" the old bus driver asked.

Abby looked back at him. "This is where I have to be," she replied. The man looked at her, confused. Abby walked into the nothingness as the sun finally started coming up. She was a girl with nothing to lose and was programmed to be evil. Abby didn't realize it yet but it made her very dangerous—more dangerous than ever before. She didn't know what the future held or if she had one. She and Hecate would take it day by day, hoping to finally find a place to permanently call home.

Printed in the United States
By Bookmasters